Five Go Adventuring Again

Enid Blyton

Hodder
Children's
Books

A division of Hodder Headline plc

First published in Great Britain in 1942
by Hodder and Stoughton

This edition 1991

10 9 8

British Library C.I.P.

Blyton, Enid
Five go adventuring again. –
(Blyton, Enid. Famous Five).
I. Title
823'.912[J]   PZ7

ISBN 0 340 54876 2

Printed and bound in Great Britain by
Cox & Wyman Ltd., Reading, Berkshire

Hodder Children's Books
a division of Hodder Headline plc
338 Euston Road
London NW1 3BH

Contents

1 Christmas holidays

It was the last week of the Christmas term, and all the girls at Gaylands School were looking forward to the Christmas Holidays. Anne sat down at the breakfast-table and picked up a letter addressed to her. .

'Hallo, look at this!' she said to her cousin Georgina, who was sitting beside her. 'A letter from Daddy – and I only had one from him and Mummy yesterday.'

'I hope it's not bad news,' said George. She would not allow anyone to call her Georgina, and now even the mistresses called her George. She really was very like a boy with her short curly hair, and her boyish ways. She looked anxiously at Anne as her cousin read the letter.

'Oh, George – we can't go home for the holidays!' said Anne, with tears in her eyes. 'Mummy's got scarlet fever – and Daddy is in quarantine for it – so they can't have us back. Isn't it just too bad?'

'Oh, I *am* sorry,' said George. She was just as disappointed for herself as for Anne, because Anne's mother had invited George, and her dog Timothy, to stay for the Christmas holidays with them. She had been promised many things she had never seen before – the pantomime, and the circus – and a big party with a fine Christmas tree! Now it wouldn't happen.

'Whatever will the two boys say?' said Anne, thinking of Julian and Dick, her two brothers. 'They won't be able to go home either.'

'Well – what are you going to do for the holidays then?' asked George. 'Won't you come and stay at Kirrin Cottage with *me*? I'm sure my mother would love to have you again. We had such fun when you came to stay for the summer hols.'

'Wait a minute – let me finish the letter and see what Daddy says,' said Anne, picking up the note again. 'Poor Mummy – I do hope she isn't feeling very ill.'

She read a few more lines and then gave such a delighted exclamation that George and the other girls waited impatiently for her to explain.

'George! We *are* to come to you again – but oh blow, blow, blow! – we've got to have a tutor for the hols, partly to look after us so that your mother doesn't have too much bother with us, and partly because both Julian and Dick have been ill with 'flu twice this term, and have got behind in their work.'

'A tutor! How sickening! That means I'll have to do lessons too, I'll bet!' said George, in dismay. 'When my mother and father see my report I guess they'll find out how little I know. After all, this is the first time I've ever been to a proper school, and there are heaps of things I don't know.'

'What horrid hols they'll be, if we have a tutor running after us all the time,' said Anne, gloomily. 'I expect I'll have quite a good report, because I've done well in the exams – but it won't be any fun for me not doing lessons with you three in the hols. Though, of course, I could go off with Timothy, I suppose. *He* won't be doing lessons!'

'Yes, he will,' said George, at once. She could not bear the idea of her beloved dog Timothy going off each morning with Anne, while she, George, sat and worked hard with Julian and Dick.

'Timothy can't do lessons, don't be silly, George,' said Anne.

'He can sit under my feet while *I'm* doing them,' said George. 'It will be a great help to feel him there. For goodness' sake eat up your sausages, Anne. We've all nearly finished. The bell will be going in a minute and you won't have had any breakfast.'

'I am glad Mummy isn't very bad,' said Anne, hurriedly finishing her letter. 'Daddy says he's written to Dick and Julian – and to your father to ask him to engage a tutor for us. Oh dash – this is an awful disappointment, isn't it? I don't mean I shan't enjoy going to Kirrin Cottage again – and seeing Kirrin Island – but after all there are no pantomimes or circuses or parties to look forward to at Kirrin.'

The end of the term came quickly. Anne and George packed up their trunks, and put on the labels, enjoying the noise and excitement of the last two days. The big school coaches rolled up to the door, and the girls clambered in.

'Off to Kirrin again!' said Anne. 'Come on, Timothy darling, you can sit between me and George.'

Gaylands School allowed the children to keep their own pets, and Timothy, George's big mongrel dog, had been a great success. Except for the time when he had run after the dustman, and dragged the dustbin away from him, all the way up the school grounds and into George's classroom, he had really behaved extremely well.

'I'm sure *you'll* have a good report, Tim,' said George, giving the dog a hug. 'We're going home again. Will you like that?'

'Woof,' said Tim, in his deep voice. He stood up, wagging his tail, and there was a squeal from the seat behind.

'George! Make Tim sit down. He's wagging my hat off!'

It was not very long before the two girls and Timothy were in London, being put into the train for Kirrin.

'I do wish the boys broke up today too,' sighed Anne. 'Then we could all have gone down to Kirrin together. That would have been fun.'

Julian and Dick broke up the next day and were to join the girls then at Kirrin Cottage. Anne was very much looking forward to seeing them again. A term was a long time to be away from one another. She had been glad to have her cousin George with her. The three of them had stayed with George in the summer, and had had some exciting adventures together on the little island off the coast. An old castle stood on the island and in the dungeons the children had made all kinds of wonderful discoveries.

'It will be lovely to go across to Kirrin Island again, George,' said Anne, as the train sped off towards the west.

'We shan't be able to,' said George. 'The sea is terribly rough round the island in the winter. It would be too dangerous to try and row there.'

'Oh, what a pity,' said Anne disappointed. 'I was looking forward to some more adventures there.'

'There won't be any adventures at Kirrin in the winter,' said George. 'It's cold down there – and when it snows we sometimes get frozen up completely – can't even walk to the village because the sea-wind blows the snow-drifts so high.'

'Oooh – that sounds rather exciting!' said Anne.

'Well, it isn't really,' said George. 'It's awfully boring – nothing to do but sit at home all day, or turn out with a spade and dig the snow away.'

It was a long time before the train reached the little station that served Kirrin. But at last it was there pulling in slowly and stopping at the tiny platform. The two girls jumped out eagerly, and looked to see if anyone had met them. Yes – there was George's mother!

'Hallo, George darling – hallo, Anne!' said George's mother, and gave both children a hug. 'Anne, I'm so sorry about your mother, but she's getting on all right, you'll be glad to know.'

'Oh, good!' said Anne. 'It's nice of you to have us, Aunt Fanny. We'll try and be good! What about Uncle Quentin? Will he mind having four children in the house in the winter-time? We won't be able to go out and leave him in peace as often as we did in the summer!'

George's father was a scientist, a very clever man, but rather frightening. He had little patience with children, and the four of them had felt very much afraid of him at times in the summer.

'Oh, your uncle is still working very hard at his book,' said Aunt Fanny. 'You know, he has been working out a secret theory – a secret idea – and putting it all into his book. He says that once it is all explained and finished, he is to take it to some high authority, and then his idea will be used for the good of the country.'

'Oh, Aunt Fanny – it does sound exciting,' said Anne. 'What's the secret?'

'I can't tell you that, silly,' said her aunt, laughing. 'Why, even I myself don't know it. Come along, now – it's cold standing here. Timothy looks very fat and well, George dear.'

'Oh Mother, he's had a marvellous time at school,'

said George. 'He really has. He chewed up the cook's old slippers . . .'

'And he chased the cat that lives in the stables every time he saw her,' said Anne.

'And he once got into the larder and ate a whole steak pie,' said George; 'and once . . .'

'Good gracious, George, I should think the school will refuse to have Timothy next term,' said her mother, in horror. 'Wasn't he well punished? I hope he was.'

'No – he wasn't,' said George, going rather red. 'You see, Mother, we are responsible for our pets and their behaviour ourselves – so if ever Timothy does anything bad *I'm* punished for it, because I haven't shut him up properly, or something like that.'

'Well, you must have had quite a lot of punishments then,' said her mother, as she drove the little pony-trap along the frosty roads. 'I really think that's rather a good idea!' There was a twinkle in her eyes as she spoke. 'I think I'll keep on with the same idea – punish you every time Timothy misbehaves himself!'

The girls laughed. They felt happy and excited. Holidays were fun. Going back to Kirrin was lovely. Tomorrow the boys would come – and then Christmas would be there!

'Good old Kirrin Cottage!' said Anne, as they came in sight of the pretty old house. 'Oh – look, there's Kirrin Island!' The two looked out to sea, where the old ruined castle stood on the little island of Kirrin – what adventures they had had there in the summer!

The girls went into the house. 'Quentin!' called George's mother. 'Quentin! The girls are here.'

Uncle Quentin came out of his study at the other side of the house. Anne thought he looked taller and darker than ever. 'And frownier!' she said to herself.

Uncle Quentin might be very clever, but Anne preferred someone jolly and smiling like her own father. She shook hands with her uncle politely, and watched George kiss him.

'Well!' said Uncle Quentin to Anne. 'I hear I've got to get a tutor for you! At least, for the two boys. My word, you *will* have to behave yourself with a tutor, I can tell you!'

This was meant to be a joke, but it didn't sound very nice to Anne and George. People you had to behave well with were usually very strict and tiresome. Both girls were glad when George's father had gone back into his study.

'Your father has been working far too hard lately,' said George's mother to her. 'He is tired out. Thank goodness his book is nearly finished. He had hoped to finish it by Christmas so that he could join in the fun and games – but now he says he can't.'

'What a pity,' said Anne, politely, though secretly she thought it was a good thing. It wouldn't be much fun having Uncle Quentin to play charades and things like that! 'Oh, Aunt Fanny, I'm so looking forward to seeing Julian and Dick – and won't they be pleased to see Tim and George? Aunt Fanny, nobody calls George Georgina at school, not even our form mistress. I was rather hoping they would, because I wanted to see what would happen when she refused to answer to Georgina! George, you liked school, didn't you?'

'Yes,' said George, 'I did. I thought I'd hate being with a lot of others, but it's fun, after all. But Mother, you won't find my report very good, I'm afraid. There were such a lot of things I was bad at because I'd never done them before.'

'Well, you'd never been to school before!' said her

mother. 'I'll explain it to your father if he gets upset. Now go along and get ready for a late tea. You must be very hungry.'

The girls went upstairs to their little room. 'I'm glad I'm not spending my hols by myself,' said George. 'I've had much more fun since I've known you and the boys. Hey, Timothy, where have you gone?'

'He's gone to smell all around the house to make sure it's his proper home!' said Anne, with a giggle. 'He wants to know if the kitchen smells the same – and the bathroom – and his basket. It must be just as exciting for him to come home for the holidays as it is for us!'

Anne was right. Timothy was thrilled to be back again. He ran round George's mother, sniffing at her legs in friendliness, pleased to see her again. He ran into the kitchen but soon came out again because someone new was there – Joanna the cook – a fat, panting person who eyed him with suspicion.

'You can come into this kitchen once a day for your dinner,' said Joanna. 'And that's all. I'm not having meat and sausages and chicken disappearing under my nose if I can help it. I know what dogs are, I do!'

Timothy ran into the scullery and sniffed round there. He ran into the dining-room and the sitting-room, and was pleased to find they had the same old smell. He put his nose to the door of the study where George's father worked, and sniffed very cautiously. He didn't mean to go in. Timothy was just as wary of George's father as the others were!

He ran upstairs to the girl's bedroom again. Where was his basket? Ah, there it was by the window-seat. Good! That meant he was to sleep in the girls' bedroom once more. He curled himself up in his basket, and thumped loudly with his tail.

'Glad to be back,' said his tail, 'glad – to – be – back!'

2 All together again

The next day the boys came back. Anne and George went to meet them with Timothy. George drove the pony-trap, and Tim sat beside her. Anne could hardly wait for the train to stop at the station. She ran along the platform, looking for Julian and Dick in the carriages that passed.

Then she saw them. They were looking out of a window at the back of the train, waving and yelling.

'Anne! Anne! Here we are! Hallo, George! Oh, there's Timothy!'

'Julian! Dick!' yelled Anne. Timothy began to bark and leap about. It was most exciting.

'Oh, Julian! It's lovely to see you both again!' cried Anne, giving her two brothers a hug each. Timothy leapt up and licked them both. He was beside himself with joy. Now he had all the children around him that he loved.

The three children and the dog stood happily together, all talking at once while the porter got the luggage out of the train. Anne suddenly remembered George. She looked round her. She was nowhere to be seen, although she had come on the station platform with Anne.

'Where's old George?' said Julian. 'I saw her here when I waved out of the window.'

'She must have gone back to the pony-trap,' said Anne. 'Tell the porter to bring your trunks out to the trap, Julian. Come along! We'll go and find George.'

George was standing by the pony, holding his head. She looked rather gloomy, Anne thought. The boys went up to her.

'Hallo, George, old thing!' cried Julian, and gave her a hug. Dick did the same.

'What's up?' asked Anne, wondering at George's sudden silence.

'I believe George felt left-out!' said Julian with a grin. 'Funny old Georgina!'

'*Don't* call me Georgina!' said the little girl fiercely. The boys laughed.

'Ah, it's the same fierce old George, all right,' said Dick, and gave the girl a friendly slap on the shoulder. 'Oh, George – it's good to see you again. Do you remember our marvellous adventures in the summer?'

George felt her awkwardness slipping away from her. She *had* felt left-out when she had seen the great welcome that the two boys gave to their small sister – but no one could sulk for long with Julian and Dick. They just wouldn't let anyone feel left-out or awkward or sulky.

The four children climbed into the trap. The porter heaved in the two trunks. There was only just room for them. Timothy sat on top of the trunks, his tail wagging nineteen to the dozen, and his tongue hanging out because he was panting with delight.

'You two girls were lucky to be able to take Tim to school with you,' said Dick, patting the big dog lovingly. 'No pets are allowed at our school. Awfully hard on those fellows who like live things.'

'Thompson Minor kept white mice,' said Julian. 'And one day they escaped and met Matron round a corner of the passage. She squealed the place down.'

The girls laughed. The boys always had funny tales to tell when they got home.

'And Kennedy keeps snails,' said Dick. 'You know, snails sleep for the winter – but Kennedy kept his in far too warm a place, and they all crawled out of their box and went up the walls. You should have heard how we laughed when the geography master asked Thompson to point out Cape Town on the map – and there was one of the snails in the very place!'

Everyone laughed again. It was so good to be all together once more. They were very much of an age – Julian was twelve. George and Dick were eleven, and Anne was ten. Holidays and Christmas time were in front of them. No wonder they laughed at everything, even the silliest little joke!

'It's good that Mummy is getting on all right, isn't it?' said Dick, as the pony went along the road at a great pace. 'I was disappointed not to go home. I must say – I did want to go to see Aladdin and the Lamp, and the circus – but still, it's good to be back at Kirrin Cottage again. I wish we could have some more exciting adventures. Not a hope of that this time, though.'

'There's one snag about these hols,' said Julian. 'And that's the tutor. I hear we've got to have one because Dick and I missed so much school this term, and we've got to take important exams next summer.'

'Yes,' said Anne. 'I wonder what he'll be like. I do hope he will be a sport. Uncle Quentin is going to choose one today.'

Julian and Dick made faces at one another. They felt sure that any tutor chosen by Uncle Quentin would be anything but a sport. Uncle Quentin's idea of a tutor would be somebody strict and gloomy and forbidding.

Never mind! He wouldn't come for a day or two. And he *might* be fun. The boys cheered up and pulled Timothy's thick coat. The dog pretended to growl and bite. *He* wasn't worried about tutors. Lucky Timothy!

They all arrived at Kirrin Cottage. The boys were really pleased to see their aunt, and rather relieved when she said that their uncle had not yet come back.

'He's gone to see two or three men who have answered the advertisement for a tutor,' she said. 'It won't be long before he's back.'

'Mother, I haven't got to do lessons in the hols too, have I?' asked George. Nothing had yet been said to her about this, and she longed to know.

'Oh yes, George,' said her mother. 'Your father has seen your report, and although it isn't really a bad one, and we certainly didn't expect a marvellous one, still it does show that you are behind your age in some things. A little extra coaching will soon help you along.'

George looked gloomy. She had expected this but it was tiresome all the same. 'Anne's the only one who won't have to do lessons,' she said.

'I'll do some too,' promised Anne. 'Perhaps not always, George, if it's a very fine day, for instance – but sometimes, just to keep you company.'

'Thanks,' said George. 'But you needn't. I shall have Timmy.'

George's mother looked doubtful about this. 'We'll have to see what the tutor says about that,' she said.

'Mother! If the tutor says I can't have Timothy in the room, I jolly well won't do holiday lessons!' began George, fiercely.

Her mother laughed. 'Well, well – here's our fierce, hot-tempered George again!' she said. 'Go along, you two boys, and wash your hands and do your hair.

You seem to have collected all the grime on the railway.'

The children and Timothy went upstairs. It was such fun to be five again. They always counted Tim as one of themselves. He went everywhere with them, and really seemed to understand every single word they said.

'I wonder what sort of a tutor Uncle Quentin will choose,' said Dick, as he scrubbed his nails. 'If only he would choose the right kind – someone jolly and full of fun, who knows that holiday lessons are sickening to have, and tries to make up for them by being a sport out of lesson-time. I suppose we'll have to work every morning.'

'Hurry up. I want my tea,' said Julian. 'Come on down, Dick. We'll know about the tutor soon enough!'

They all went down together, and sat round the table. Joanna the cook had made a lovely lot of buns and a great big cake. There was not much left of either by the time the four children had finished!

Uncle Quentin returned just as they were finishing. He seemed rather pleased with himself. He shook hands with the two boys and asked them if they had had a good term.

'Did you get a tutor, Uncle Quentin?' asked Anne, who could see that everyone was simply bursting to know this.

'Ah – yes, I did,' said her uncle. He sat down, while Aunt Fanny poured him out a cup of tea. 'I interviewed three applicants, and had almost chosen the last one, when another fellow came in, all in a hurry. Said he had only just seen the advertisement, and hoped he wasn't too late.'

'Did you choose him?' asked Dick.

'I did,' said his uncle. 'He seemed a most intelligent fellow. Even knew about me and my work! And he had the most wonderful letters of recommendation.'

'I don't think the children need to know all these details,' murmured Aunt Fanny. 'Anyway – you asked him to come?'

'Oh yes,' said Uncle Quentin. 'He's a good bit older than the others – they were rather young fellows – this one seems very responsible and intelligent. I'm sure you'll like him, Fanny. He'll fit in here very well. I feel I would like to have him to talk to me sometimes in the evening.'

The children couldn't help feeling that the new tutor sounded rather alarming. Their uncle smiled at the gloomy faces.

'You'll like Mr Roland,' he said. 'He knows how to handle youngsters – knows he's got to be very firm, and to see that you know a good bit more at the end of the holidays than you did at the beginning.'

This sounded even more alarming. All four children wished heartily that Aunt Fanny had been to choose the tutor, and not Uncle Quentin.

'When is he coming?' asked George.

'Tomorrow,' said her father. 'You can all go to meet him at the station. That will make a nice welcome for him.'

'We *had* thought of taking the bus and going to do a bit of Christmas shopping,' said Julian, seeing Anne looked very disappointed.

'Oh, no, you must certainly go and meet Mr Roland,' said his uncle. 'I told him you would. And mind you, you four – no nonsense with him! You've to do as you're told, and you must work hard with him, because your father is paying very high fees for his coaching. I'm paying a third, because I want him to coach George a little too – so George, you must do your best.'

'I'll try,' said George. 'If he's nice, I'll do my very best.'

'You'll do your best whether you think him nice or not!' said her father, frowning. 'He will arrive by the ten-thirty train. Be sure to be there in time.'

'I do hope he won't be too strict,' said Dick, that evening, when the five of them were alone for a minute or two. 'It's going to spoil the hols, if we have someone down on us all the time. And I do hope he'll like Timothy.'

George looked up at once. 'Like Timothy!' she said. 'Of course he'll like Timothy! How couldn't he?'

'Well – your father didn't like Timothy very much last summer,' said Dick. 'I don't see how anyone could *dislike* darling Tim – but there are people who don't like dogs, you know, George.'

'If Mr Roland doesn't like Timothy, I'll not do a single thing for him,' said George. 'Not one single thing!'

'She's gone all fierce again!' said Dick, with a laugh. 'My word – the sparks will fly if Mr Roland dares to dislike our Timothy!'

3 The new tutor

Next morning the sun was out, all the sea-mist that had hung about for the last two days had disappeared, and Kirrin Island showed plainly at the mouth of Kirrin Bay. The children stared longingly at the ruined castle on it.

'I do wish we could get over to the castle,' said Dick. 'It looks quite calm enough, George.'

'It's very rough by the island,' said George. 'It always is at this time of year. I know Mother wouldn't let us go.'

'It's a lovely island, and it's all our own!' said Anne. 'You said you would share it with us for ever and ever, didn't you, George?'

'Yes, I did,' said George. 'And so I will, dungeons and all. Come on – we must get the trap out. We shall be late meeting the train if we stand here all day looking at the island.'

They got the pony and trap and set off down the hard lanes. Kirrin Island disappeared behind the cliffs as they turned inland to the station.

'Did all this land round about belong to your family once upon a time?' asked Julian.

'Yes, all of it,' said George. 'Now we don't own anything except Kirrin Island, our own house and that farm away over there – Kirrin Farm.'

She pointed with her whip. The children saw a fine

old farmhouse standing on a hill a good way off, over the heather-clad common.

'Who lives there?' asked Julian.

'Oh, an old farmer and his wife,' said George. 'They were nice to me when I was smaller. We'll go over there one day, if you like. Mother says they don't make the farm pay any more, and in the summertime they take in people who want a holiday.'

'Listen! That's the train whistling in the tunnel!' said Julian, suddenly. 'Buck up, for goodness' sake, George. We shan't be there in time!'

The four children and Timothy looked at the train coming out of the tunnel and drawing in at the station. The pony cantered along swiftly. They would be just in time.

'Who's going on to the platform to meet him?' asked George, as they drew into the little station yard. 'I'm not. I must look after Tim and the pony.'

'I don't want to,' said Anne. 'I'll stay with George.'

'Well, we'd better go, then,' said Julian, and he and Dick leapt out of the trap. They ran on to the platform just as the train pulled up.

Not many people got out. A woman clambered out with a basket. A young man leapt out, whistling, the son of the baker in the village. An old man climbed down with difficulty. The tutor could be none of those!

Then, right at the front of the train, rather an odd-looking man got out. He was short and burly, and he had a beard rather like a sailor. His eyes were piercingly blue, and his thick hair was sprinkled with grey. He glanced up and down the platform, and then beckoned to the porter.

'That must be Mr Roland,' said Julian to Dick.

'Come on – let's ask him. There's no one else it could be.'

The boys went up to the bearded man. 'Are you Mr Roland, sir?' he asked.

'I am,' said the man. 'I suppose you are Julian and Dick?'

'Yes, sir,' answered the boys together. 'We brought the pony-trap for your luggage.'

'Oh, fine,' said Mr Roland. His bright blue eyes looked the boys up and down, and he smiled. Julian and Dick liked him. He seemed sensible and jolly.

'Are the other two here as well?' said Mr Roland, walking down the platform, with the porter trailing behind with his luggage.

'Yes – George and Anne are outside with the trap,' said Julian.

'George and Anne,' said Mr Roland, in a puzzled voice. 'I thought the others were girls. I didn't know there was a third boy.'

'Oh, George is a girl,' said Dick, with a laugh. 'Her real name is Georgina.'

'And a very nice name, too,' said Mr Roland.

'George doesn't think so,' said Julian. 'She won't answer if she's called Georgina. You'd better call her George, sir!'

'Really?' said Mr Roland, in rather a chilly tone. Julian took a glance at him.

'Not quite so jolly as he looks!' thought the boy.

'Tim's out there too,' said Dick.

'Oh – and is Tim a boy or a girl?' inquired Mr Roland, cautiously.

'A dog, sir!' said Dick, with a grin.

Mr Roland seemed rather taken aback. 'A dog?' he said. 'I didn't know there was a dog in the household. Your uncle said nothing to me about a dog.'

'Don't you like dogs?' asked Julian, in surprise.

'No,' said Mr Roland, shortly. 'But I dare say your dog won't worry me much. Hallo, hallo – so here are the little girls! How do you do?'

George was not very pleased at being called a little girl. For one thing she hated to be spoken of as little, and for another thing she always tried to be a boy. She held out her hand to Mr Roland and said nothing. Anne smiled at him, and Mr Roland thought she was much the nicer of the two.

'Tim! Shake hands with Mr Roland!' said Julian to Timothy. This was one of Tim's really good tricks. He could hold out his right paw in a very polite manner. Mr Roland looked down at the big dog, and Tim looked back at him.

Then, very slowly and deliberately, Timothy turned his back on Mr Roland and climbed up into the pony-trap! Usually he put out his paw at once when told to, and the children stared at him in amazement.

'Timothy! What's come over you?' cried Dick. Tim put his ears down and did not move.

'He doesn't like you,' said George, looking at Mr Roland. 'That's very strange. He usually likes people. But perhaps you don't like dogs?'

'No, I don't, as a matter of fact,' said Mr Roland. 'I was once very badly bitten as a boy, and somehow or other I've never managed to like dogs since. But I dare say your Tim will take to me sooner or later.'

They all got into the trap. It was a tight squeeze. Timothy looked at Mr Roland's ankles as if he would rather like to nibble them. Anne laughed.

'Tim *is* behaving strangely!' she said. 'It's a good thing you haven't come to teach him, Mr Roland!' She smiled up at the tutor, and he smiled back, showing very white teeth. His eyes were as brilliant a blue as George's.

Anne liked him. He joked with the boys as they drove him, and both of them began to feel that their Uncle Quentin hadn't made such a bad choice after all.

Only George said nothing. She sensed that the tutor disliked Timothy, and George was not prepared to like anyone who didn't take to Timothy at first sight. She thought it was very peculiar too, that Tim would not shake paws with the tutor. 'He's a clever dog,' she thought. 'He knows Mr Roland doesn't like him, so he won't shake hands. I don't blame you, Tim darling, I wouldn't shake hands with anyone who didn't like *me*!'

Mr Roland was shown up to his room when he arrived. Aunt Fanny came down and spoke to the children. 'Well! He seems very nice, youngish and jolly.'

'Youngish!' exclaimed Julian. 'Why, he's awfully old! Must be forty at the very least!'

Aunt Fanny laughed. 'Does he seem so old to you?' she said. 'Well, old or not, he'll be quite nice to you, I'm sure.'

'Aunt Fanny, we shan't begin lessons until after Christmas, shall we?' asked Julian, anxiously.

'Of course you will!' said his aunt. 'It is almost a week till Christmas – you don't suppose we have asked Mr Roland to come and do nothing till Christmas is over, do you?'

The children groaned. 'We wanted to do some Christmas shopping,' said Anne.

'Well, you can do that in the afternoon,' said her aunt. 'You will only do lessons in the morning, for three hours. That won't hurt any of you!'

The new tutor came downstairs at that moment,

and Aunt Fanny took him to see Uncle Quentin. She came out after a while, looking very pleased.

'Mr Roland will be nice company for your uncle,' she said to Julian. 'I think they will get on very well together. Mr Roland seems to understand quite a bit about your uncle's work.'

'Let's hope he spends most of his time with him then!' said George, in a low voice.

'Come on out for a walk,' said Dick. 'It's so fine today. We shan't have lessons this morning, shall we, Aunt Fanny?'

'Oh, no,' said his aunt. 'You'll begin tomorrow. Go for a walk now, all of you – we shan't often get sunny days like this!'

'Let's go over to Kirrin Farm,' said Julian. 'It looks such a nice place. Show us the way, George.'

'Right!' said George. She whistled to Timothy, and he came bounding up. The five of them set off together, going down the lane, and then on to a rough road over the common that led to the farm on the distant hill.

It was lovely walking in the December sun. Their feet rang on the frosty path, and Tim's blunt claws made quite a noise as he pattered up and down, overjoyed at being with his four friends again.

After a good long walk across the common the children came to the farmhouse. It was built of white stone, and stood strong and lovely on the hillside. George opened the farm-gate and went into the farm-yard. She kept her hand on Tim's collar for there were two farm-dogs somewhere about.

Someone clattered round the barn near-by. It was an old man, and George hailed him loudly.

'Hallo, Mr Sanders! How are you?'

'Why, if it isn't Master George!' said the old fellow

with a grin. George grinned too. She loved being called Master instead of Miss.

'These are my cousins,' shouted George. She turned to the others. 'He's deaf,' she said. 'You'll have to shout to make him hear.'

'I'm Julian,' said Julian in a loud voice and the others said their names too. The farmer beamed at them.

'You come along in and see the Missis,' he said. 'She'll be rare pleased to see you all. We've known Master George since she was a baby, and we knew her mother when *she* was a baby too, and we knew her granny as well.'

'You must be very, very old,' said Anne.

The farmer smiled down at her.

'As old as my tongue and a little older than my teeth!' he said, chuckling. 'Come away in now.'

They all went into the big, warm farmhouse kitchen, where a little old woman, as lively as a bantam hen, was bustling about. She was just as pleased to see the four children as her husband was.

'Well, there now!' she said. 'I haven't seen you for months, Master George. I did hear that you'd gone away to school.'

'Yes, I did,' said George. 'But I'm home for the holidays now. Does it matter if I let Timothy loose, Mrs Sanders? I think he'll be friendly if your dogs are, too.'

'Yes, you let him loose,' said the old lady. 'He'll have a fine time in the farmyard with Ben and Rikky. Now what would you like to drink? Hot milk? Cocoa? Coffee? And I've some new shortbread baked yesterday. You shall have some of that.'

'Ah, my wife's very busy this week, cooking up all sorts of things,' said the old farmer, as his wife bustled off to the larder. 'We've company this Christmas!'

'Have you?' said George, surprised, for she knew that the old pair had never had any children of their own. 'Who is coming? Anyone I know?'

'Two artists from London Town!' said the old farmer. 'Wrote and asked us to take them for three weeks over Christmas – and offered us good money too. So my old wife's as busy as a bee.'

'Are they going to paint pictures?' asked Julian, who rather fancied himself as an artist, too. 'I wonder if I could come and talk to them some day. I'm rather good at pictures myself. They might give me a few hints.'

'You come along whenever you like,' said old Mrs Sanders, making cocoa in a big jug. She set out a plate of most delicious-looking shortbreads, and the children ate them hungrily.

'I should think the two artists will be rather lonely down here, in the depths of the country at Christmas-time,' said George. 'Do they know anyone?'

'They say they don't know a soul,' said Mrs Sanders. 'But there – artists can be peculiar folk. I've had some here before. They seemed to like mooning about all alone. These two will be happy enough, I'll be bound.'

'They should be, with all the good things you're cooking up for them,' said her old husband. 'Well, I must be out after the sheep. Good–day to you, young-sters. Come again and see us sometime.'

He went out. Old Mrs Sanders chattered on to the children as she bustled about the big kitchen. Timothy ran in and settled down on the rug by the fire.

He suddenly saw a tabby cat slinking along by the wall, all her hairs on end with fear of the strange dog. He gave a delighted wuff and sprang at the cat. She fled out of the kitchen into the old panelled hall. Tim flew after her, taking no notice at all of George's stern shout.

The cat tried to leap on top of an old grandfather clock in the hall. With a joyous bark Tim sprang too. He flung himself against a polished panel – and then a most extraordinary thing happened!

The panel disappeared – and a dark hole showed in the old wall! George, who had followed Tim out into the hall, gave a loud cry of surprise. 'Look! Mrs Sanders, come and look!'

4 An exciting discovery

Old Mrs Sanders and the other three children rushed out into the hall when they heard George's shout.

'What's up?' cried Julian. 'What's happened?'

'Tim sprang at the cat, missed her, and fell hard against the panelled wall,' said George, 'and the panel moved, and look – there's a hole in the wall!'

'It's a secret panel!' cried Dick, in excitement, peering into the hole. 'Golly! Did you know there was one here, Mrs Sanders?'

'Oh yes,' said the old lady. 'This house is full of funny things like that. I'm very careful when I polish that panel, because if I rub too hard in the top corner, it always slides back.'

'What's behind the panel?' asked Julian. The hole was only about the width of his head, and when he stuck his head inside, he could see only darkness. The wall itself was about eight inches behind the panelling, and was of stone.

'Get a candle, do get a candle!' said Anne, thrilled. 'You haven't got a torch, have you, Mrs Sanders?'

'No,' said the old woman. 'But you can get a candle if you like. There's one on the kitchen mantelpiece.'

Anne shot off to get it. Julian lit it and put it into the hole behind the panel. The others pushed against him to try and peep inside.

'Don't,' said Julian, impatiently. 'Wait your turn, sillies! Let me have a look.'

He had a good look, but there didn't really seem anything to see. It was all darkness behind, and stone wall. He gave the candle to Dick, and then each of the children had a turn at peeping. Old Mrs Sanders had gone back to the kitchen. She was used to the sliding panel!

'She said this house was full of strange things like that,' said Anne. 'What other things are there, do you think? Let's ask her.'

They slid the panel back into place and went to find Mrs Sanders. 'Mrs Sanders, what other funny things are there in Kirrin Farmhouse?' asked Julian.

'There's a cupboard upstairs with a false back,' said Mrs Sanders. 'Don't look so excited! There's nothing in it at all! And there's a big stone over there by the fireplace that pulls up to show a hidey-hole. I suppose in the old days people wanted good hiding-places for things.'

The children ran to the stone she pointed out. It had an iron ring in it, and was easily pulled up. Below was a hollowed-out place, big enough to take a small box. It was empty now, but all the same it looked exciting.

'Where's the cupboard?' asked Julian.

'My old legs are too tired to go traipsing upstairs this morning,' said the farmer's wife. 'But you can go yourselves. Up the stairs, turn to the right, and go into the second door you see. The cupboard is at the farther end. Open the door and feel about at the bottom till you come across a dent in the wood. Press it hard, and the false back slides to the side.'

The four children and Timothy ran upstairs as fast as they could, munching shortbread as they went. This really was a very exciting morning!

They found the cupboard and opened the door. All four went down on hands and knees to press round the bottom of the cupboard to find the dented place. Anne found it.

'I've got it!' she cried. She pressed hard, but her little fingers were not strong enough to work the mechanism of the sliding back. Julian had to help her.

There was a creaking noise, and the children saw the false back of the cupboard sliding sideways. A big space showed behind, large enough to take a fairly thin man.

'A jolly good hiding-place,' said Julian. 'Anyone could hide there and no one would ever know!'

'I'll get in and you shut me up,' said Dick. 'It would be exciting.'

He got into the space. Julian slid the back across, and Dick could no longer be seen!

'Bit of a tight fit!' he called. 'And awfully dark! Let me out again.'

The children all took turns at going into the space behind the back of the cupboard and being shut up. Anne didn't like it very much.

They went down to the warm kitchen again. 'It's a most exciting cupboard, Mrs Sanders,' said Julian. 'I do wish we lived in a house like this, full of secrets!'

'Can we come and play in that cupboard again?' asked George.

'No, I'm afraid you can't, George,' said Mrs Sanders. 'That room where the cupboard is, is one the two gentlemen are going to have.'

'Oh!' said Julian, disappointed. 'Shall you tell them about the sliding back, Mrs Sanders?'

'I don't expect so,' said the old lady. 'It's only you children that get excited about things like that, bless you. Two gentlemen wouldn't think twice about it.'

'How funny grown-ups are!' said Anne, puzzled. 'I'm quite certain I shall be thrilled to see a sliding panel or a trapdoor even when I'm a hundred.'

'Same here,' said Dick. 'Could I just go and look into the sliding panel in the hall once more, Mrs Sanders? I'll take the candle.'

Dick never knew why he suddenly wanted to have another look. It was just an idea he had. The others didn't bother to go with him, for there really was nothing to see behind the panelling except the old stone wall.

Dick took the candle and went into the hall. He pressed on the panel at the top and it slid back. He put the candle inside and had another good look. There was nothing at all to be seen. Dick took out his head and put in his arm, stretching along the wall as far as his hand would reach. He was just about to take it back when his fingers found a hole in the wall.

'Funny!' said Dick. 'Why should there be a hole in the stone wall just there?'

He stuck in his finger and thumb and worked them about. He felt a little ridge inside the wall, rather like a bird's perch, and was able to get hold of it. He wriggled his fingers about the perch, but nothing happened. Then he got a good hold and pulled.

The stone came right out! Dick was so surprised that he let go the heavy stone and it fell to the ground behind the panelling with a crash!

The noise brought the others out into the hall. 'Whatever are you doing, Dick?' said Julian. 'Have you broken something?'

'No,' said Dick, his face reddening with excitement. 'I say – I put my hand in here – and found a hole in one of the stones the wall is made of – and I got hold of a sort of ridge with my finger and thumb and pulled. The stone came right out, and I got such a surprise I let go. It fell, and that's what you heard!'

'Golly!' said Julian, trying to push Dick away from the open panel. 'Let me see.'

'No, Julian,' said Dick, pushing him away. 'This is *my* discovery. Wait till I see if I can feel anything in the hole. It's difficult to get at!'

The others waited impatiently. Julian could hardly prevent himself from pushing Dick right away. Dick put his arm in as far as he could, and curved his hand round to get into the space behind where the stone had been. His fingers felt about and he closed them round something that felt like a book. Cautiously and carefully he brought it out.

'An old book!' he said.

'What's in it?' cried Anne.

They turned the pages carefully. They were so dry and brittle that some of them fell into dust.

'I think it's a book of recipes,' said Anne, as her sharp eyes read a few words in the old brown, faded handwriting. 'Let's take it to Mrs Sanders.'

The children carried the book to the old lady. She laughed at their beaming faces. She took the book and looked at it, not at all excited.

'Yes,' she said. 'It's a book of recipes, that's all it is. See the name in the front – Alice Mary Sanders – that must have been my husband's great-grandmother. She was famous for her medicines, I know. It was said she could cure any ill in man or animal, no matter what it was.'

'It's a pity it's so hard to read her writing,' said Julian, disappointed. 'The whole book is falling to pieces too. It must be very old.'

'Do you think there's anything else in that hidy-hole?' asked Anne. 'Julian, you go and put *your* arm in, it's longer than Dick's.'

'There didn't seem to be anything else at all,' said

Dick. 'It's a very small place – just a few inches of hollow space behind that brick or stone that fell down.'

'Well, I'll just put my hand in and see,' said Julian. They all went back into the hall. Julian put his arm into the open panel, and slid it along the wall to where the stone had fallen out. His hand went into the space there, and his long fingers groped about, feeling for anything else that might be there.

There was something else, something soft and flat that felt like leather. Eagerly the boy's fingers closed over it and he drew it out carefully, half afraid that it might fall to pieces with age.

'I've got something!' he said, his eyes gleaming brightly. 'Look – what is it?'

The others crowded round. 'It's rather like Daddy's tobacco pouch,' said Anne, feeling it. 'The same shape. Is there anything inside?'

It was a tobacco pouch, very dark brown, made of soft leather and very much worn. Carefully Julian undid the flap, and unrolled the leather.

A few bits of black tobacco were still in the pouch – but there was something else, too! Tightly rolled up in the last bit of pouch was a piece of linen. Julian took it out and unrolled it. He put it flat on the hall-table.

The children stared at it. There were marks and signs on the linen, done in black ink that had hardly faded. But the four of them could not make head or tail of the marks.

'It's not a map,' said Julian. 'It seems a sort of code, or something. I do wonder what it means. I wish we could make it out. It must be some sort of secret.'

The children stared at the piece of linen, very thrilled. It was so old – and contained some kind of secret. Whatever could it be?

They ran to show it to Mrs Sanders. She was studying the old recipe book, and her face glowed with pleasure as she raised it to look at the excited children.

'This book's a wonder!' she said. 'I can hardly read the writing, but here's a recipe for backache. I shall try it myself. My back aches so much at the end of the day. Now, you listen . . .'

But the children didn't want to listen to recipes for backache. They pushed the piece of linen on to Mrs Sanders's lap.

'Look! What's this about, Mrs Sanders? Do you know? We found it in a kind of tobacco pouch in that place behind the panel.'

Mrs Sanders took off her glasses, polished them, and put them on again. She looked carefully at the piece of linen with its strange marks.

She shook her head. 'No – this doesn't make any sense to me. And what's this now? – it looks like an old tobacco pouch. Ah, my John would like that, I guess. He's got such an old one that it won't hold his tobacco any more! This is old too – but there's a lot of wear in it yet.'

'Mrs Sanders, do you want this piece of linen too?' asked Julian, anxiously. He was longing to take it home and study it. He felt certain there was some kind of exciting secret hidden there, and he could not bear the thought of leaving it with Mrs Sanders.

'You take it, Julian, if you want it,' said Mrs Sanders, with a laugh. 'I'll keep the recipes for myself, and John shall have the pouch. You can have the old rag if you want it, though it beats me why you think it's so fascinating! Ah, here's John!'

She raised her voice and shouted to the deaf old man. 'Hey, John, here's a tobacco pouch for you. The children found it somewhere behind that panel that opens in the hall.'

John took it and fingered it. 'It's a strange one,' he said, 'but better than mine. Well, youngsters, I don't want to hurry you, but it's one o'clock now, and you'd better be going if it's near your dinner-time!'

'Gracious!' said Julian. 'We shall be late! Goodbye, Mrs Sanders, and thanks awfully for the shortbread and this old rag. We'll try our best to make out what's on it and tell you. Hurry, everyone! Where's Tim? Come on, Timothy, we're late!'

The five of them ran off quickly. They really were late, and had to run most of the way, which meant that it was difficult to talk. But they were so excited about their morning that they panted remarks to one another as they went.

'I wonder what this old rag says!' panted Julian. 'I mean to find out. I'm sure it's something mysterious.'

'Shall we tell anyone?' asked Dick.

'No!' said George. 'Let's keep it a secret.'

'If Anne starts to give away anything, kick her under the table, like we did last summer,' said Julian, with a grin. Poor Anne always found it difficult to keep a secret, and often had to be nudged or kicked when she began to give things away.

'I won't say a word,' said Anne, indignantly. 'And don't you dare to kick me. It only makes me cry out and then the grown-ups want to know why.'

'We'll have a good old puzzle over this piece of linen after dinner,' said Julian. 'I bet we'll find out what it says, if we really make up our minds to!'

'Here we are,' said George. 'Not too late. Hallo, Mother! We won't be a minute washing our hands! We've had a lovely time.'

5   An unpleasant walk

After dinner the four children went upstairs to the boys' bedroom and spread out the bit of linen on a table there. There were words here and there, scrawled in rough printing. There was the sign of a compass, with E marked clearly for East. There were eight rough squares, and in one of them, right in the middle, was a cross. It was all very mysterious.

'You know, I believe these words are Latin,' said Julian, trying to make them out. 'But I can't read them properly. And I expect if I *could* read them, I wouldn't know what they meant. I wish we knew someone who could read Latin like this.'

'Could your father, George?' asked Anne.

'I expect so,' said George. But nobody wanted to ask George's father. He might take the curious old rag away. He might forget all about it, he might even burn it. Scientists were such peculiar people.

'What about Mr Roland?' said Dick. 'He's a tutor. He knows Latin.'

'We won't ask him till we know a bit more about him,' said Julian, cautiously. 'He *seems* jolly and nice – but you never know. Oh, blow – I wish we could make this out, I really do.'

'There are two words at the top,' said Dick, and he tried to spell them out. 'VIA OCCULTA.' 'What do you think they could mean, Julian?'

'Well – the only thing I can think of that they can

mean is – Secret Way, or something like that,' said
Julian, screwing up his forehead into a frown.

'Secret Way!' said Anne, her eyes shining. 'Oh, I
hope it's that! Secret Way! How exciting. What sort of
secret way would it be, Julian?'

'How do I know, Anne, silly?' said Julian. 'I don't
even know that the words are meant to mean "Secret
Way". It's really a guess on my part.'

'If they did mean that – the linen might have direc-
tions to find the Secret Way, whatever it is,' said Dick.
'Oh Julian, isn't it exasperating that we can't read it?
Do, do try. You know more Latin than I do.'

'It's so hard to read the funny old letters,' said Julian,
trying again. 'No – it's no good at all. I can't make
them out.'

Steps came up the stairs, and the door opened. Mr
Roland looked in.

'Hallo, hallo!' he said. 'I wondered where you all
were. What about a walk over the cliffs?'

'We'll come,' said Julian, rolling up the old rag.

'What have you got there? Anything interesting?'
asked Mr Roland.

'It's a –' began Anne, and at once all the others began
to talk, afraid that Anne was going to give the secret
away.

'It's a wonderful afternoon for a walk.'

'Come on, let's get our things on!'

'Tim, Tim, where are you?' George gave a piercing
whistle. Tim was under the bed and came bounding
out. Anne went red as she guessed why all the others
had interrupted her so quickly.

'Idiot,' said Julian, under his breath. 'Baby.'

Fortunately Mr Roland said no more about the piece
of linen he had seen Julian rolling up. He was looking
at Tim.

'I suppose he must come,' he said. George stared at him in indignation.

'Of course he must!' she said. 'We never never go anywhere without Timothy.'

Mr Roland went downstairs, and the children got ready to go out. George was scowling. The very idea of leaving Tim behind made her angry.

'You nearly gave our secret away, you silly,' said Dick to Anne.

'I didn't think,' said the little girl, looking ashamed of herself. 'Anyway, Mr Roland seems very nice. I think we might ask him if he could help us to understand those funny words.'

'You leave that to me to decide,' said Julian, crossly. 'Now don't you dare to say a word.'

They all set out, Timothy too. Mr Roland need not have worried about the dog, for Timothy would not go near him. It was very strange, really. He kept away from the tutor, and took not the slightest notice of him even when Mr Roland spoke to him.

'He's not usually like that,' said Dick. 'He's a most friendly dog, really.'

'Well, as I've got to live in the same house with him, I must try and make him friends with me,' said the tutor. 'Hi, Timothy! Come here! I've got a biscuit in my pocket.'

Timothy pricked up his ears at the word 'biscuit', but did not even look towards Mr Roland. He put his tail down and went to George. She patted him.

'If he doesn't like anyone, not even a biscuit or a bone will make him go to them when he is called,' she said.

Mr Roland gave it up. He put the biscuit back into his pocket. 'He's a peculiar-looking dog, isn't he?' he said. 'A terrible mongrel! I must say I prefer well-bred dogs.'

George went purple in the face. 'He's *not* peculiar-looking!' she spluttered. 'He's not nearly so peculiar-looking as you! He's not a terrible mongrel. He's the best dog in the world!'

'I think you are being a little rude,' said Mr Roland, stiffly. 'I don't allow my pupils to be cheeky, Georgina.'

Calling her Georgina made George still more furious. She lagged behind with Tim, looking as black as a thundercloud. The others felt uncomfortable. They knew what tempers George got into, and how difficult she could be. She had been so much better and happier since the summer, when they had come to stay for the first time. They did hope she wasn't going to be silly and get into rows. It would spoil the Christmas holidays.

Mr Roland took no more notice of George. He did not speak to her, but strode on ahead with the others, doing his best to be jolly. He could really be very funny, and the boys began to laugh at him. He took Anne's hand, and the little girl jumped along beside him, enjoying the walk.

Julian felt sorry for George. It wasn't nice to be left out of things, and he knew how George hated anything like that. He wondered if he dared to put in a good word for her. It might make things easier.

'Mr Roland, sir,' he began. 'Could you call my cousin by the name she likes – George – she simply hates Georgina. And she's very fond of Tim. She can't bear anyone to say horrid things about him.'

Mr Roland looked surprised. 'My dear boy, I am sure you mean well,' he said, in rather a dry sort of voice, 'but I hardly think I want your advice about any

of my pupils. I shall follow my own wishes in my
treatment of Georgina, not yours. I want to be friends
with you all, and I am sure we shall be – but Georgina
has got to be sensible, as you three are.'

Julian felt rather squashed. He went red and looked
at Dick. Dick gave him a squeeze on his arm. The boys
knew George could be silly and difficult, especially if
anyone didn't like her beloved dog – but they thought
Mr Roland might try to be a bit more understanding
too. Dick slipped behind and walked with George.

'You needn't walk with me,' said George at once,
her blue eyes glinting. 'Walk with your friend Mr
Roland.'

'He isn't my friend,' said Dick. 'Don't be silly.'

'I'm not silly,' said George, in a tight sort of voice. 'I
heard you all laughing and joking with him. You go
on and have a good laugh again. I've got Timothy.'

'George, it's Christmas holidays,' said Dick. 'Do
let's all be friends. Do. Don't let's spoil Christmas.'

'I can't like anyone who doesn't like Tim,' said
George, obstinately.

'Well, after all, Mr Roland did offer him a biscuit,'
said Dick, trying to make peace as hard as he could.

George said nothing. Her small face looked fierce.
Dick tried again.

'George! Promise to try and be nice till Christmas is
over, anyway. Don't let's spoil Christmas, for goodness' sake! Come on, George.'

'All right,' said George, at last. 'I'll try.'

'Come and walk with us then,' said Dick. So George
caught up the others, and tried not to look too sulky.
Mr Roland guessed that Dick had been trying to make
George behave, and he included her in his talk. He
could not make her laugh, but she did at least answer
politely.

'Is that Kirrin Farmhouse?' asked Mr Roland, as they came in sight of the farm.

'Yes. Do you know it?' asked Julian, in surprise.

'No, no,' said Mr Roland, at once, 'I've heard of it, and wondered if that was the place.'

'We went there this morning,' said Anne. 'It's an exciting place.' She looked at the others, wondering if they would mind if she said anything about the things they had seen that morning. Julian thought for a moment. After all, it couldn't matter telling him about the stone in the kitchen and the false back to the cupboard. Mrs Sanders would tell anyone that. He could speak about the sliding panel in the hall too, and say they had found an old recipe book there. He did not need to say anything about the old bit of marked linen.

So he told their tutor about the exciting things there had been at the old farmhouse, but said nothing at all about the linen and its strange markings. Mr Roland listened with the greatest interest.

'This is all very remarkable,' he said. 'Very remarkable indeed. Most interesting. You say the old couple live there quite alone?'

'Well, they are having two people to stay over Christmas,' said Dick. 'Artists. Julian thought he would go over and talk to them. He can paint awfully well, you know.'

'Can he really?' said Mr Roland. 'Well, he must show me some of his pictures. But I don't think he'd better go and worry the artists at the farmhouse. They might not like it.'

This remark made Julian feel obstinate. He made up his mind at once that he *would* go and talk to the two artists when he got the chance!

It was quite a pleasant walk on the whole except that

George was quiet, and Timothy would not go anywhere near Mr Roland. When they came to a frozen
pond Dick threw sticks on it for Tim to fetch. It was so
funny to see him go slithering about on his long legs,
trying to run properly!

Everyone threw sticks for the dog, and Tim fetched
all the sticks except Mr Roland's. When the tutor
threw a stick the dog looked at it and took no more
notice. It was almost as if he had said, 'What, *your*
stick! No, thank you!'

'Now, home we go,' said Mr Roland, trying not to
look annoyed with Tim. 'We shall just be in time for
tea!'

6   *Lessons with Mr Roland*

Next morning the children felt a little gloomy. Lessons! How horrid in the holidays! Still, Mr Roland wasn't so bad. The children had not had him with them in the sitting-room the night before, because he had gone to talk to their uncle. So they were able to get out the mysterious bit of linen again and pore over it.

But it wasn't a bit of good. Nobody could make anything of it at all. Secret Way! What did it mean? Was it really directions for a Secret Way? And where was the way, and why was it secret? It was most exasperating not to be able to find out.

'I really feel we'll have to ask someone soon,' Julian had said with a sigh. 'I can't bear this mystery much longer. I keep on and on thinking of it.'

He had dreamt of it too that night, and now it was morning, with lessons ahead. He wondered what lesson Mr Roland would take – Latin perhaps. Then he could ask him what the words 'VIA OCCULTA' meant.

Mr Roland had seen all their reports and had noted the subjects they were weak in. One was Latin, and another was French. Maths were very weak in both Dick's report and George's. Both children must be helped on in those. Geometry was Julian's weakest spot.

Anne was not supposed to need any coaching. 'But if you like to come along and join us, I'll give you some painting to do,' said Mr Roland, his blue eyes twinkling at her. He liked Anne. She was not difficult and sulky like George.

Anne loved painting. 'Oh, yes,' she said, happily, 'I'd love to do some painting. I can paint flowers, Mr Roland. I'll paint you some red poppies and blue cornflowers out of my head.'

'We will start at half-past nine,' said Mr Roland. 'We are to work in the sitting-room. Take your school-books there, and be ready punctually.'

So all the children were there, sitting round a table, their books in front of them, at half-past nine. Anne had some painting water and her painting-box. The others looked at her enviously. Lucky Anne, to be doing painting while they worked hard at difficult things like Latin and Maths!

'Where's Timothy?' asked Julian in a low voice, as they waited for their tutor to come in.

'Under the table,' said George, defiantly. 'I'm sure he'll lie still. Don't any of you say anything about him. I want him there. I'm not going to do lessons without Tim here.'

'I don't see why he shouldn't be here with us,' said Dick. 'He's very very good. Sh! Here comes Mr Roland.'

The tutor came in, his black beard bristling round his mouth and chin. His eyes looked very piercing in the pale winter sunlight that filtered into the room. He told the children to sit down.

'I'll have a look at your exercise books first,' he said, 'and see what you were doing last term. You come first, Julian.'

Soon the little class were working quietly together. Anne was very busy painting a bright picture of poppies and cornflowers. Mr Roland admired it very much. Anne thought he really was very nice.

Suddenly there was a huge sigh from under the table. It was Tim, tired of lying so still. Mr Roland looked up, surprised. George at once sighed heavily, hoping that Mr Roland would think it was she who had sighed before.

'You sound tired, Georgina,' said Mr Roland. 'You shall all have a little break at eleven.'

George frowned. She hated being called Georgina. She put her foot cautiously on Timothy to warn him not to make any more noises. Tim licked her foot.

After a while, just when the class was at its very quietest, Tim felt a great wish to scratch himself very hard on his back. He got up. He sat down again with a thump, gave a grunt, and began to scratch himself furiously. The children all began to make noises to hide the sounds that Tim was making.

George clattered her feet on the floor. Julian began to cough, and let one of his books slip to the ground. Dick jiggled the table and spoke to Mr Roland.

'Oh dear, this sum is so hard; it really is! I keep doing it and doing it, and it simply *won't* come right!'

'Why all this sudden noise?' said Mr Roland in surprise. 'Stop tapping the floor with your feet, Georgina.'

Tim settled down quietly again. The children gave a sigh of relief. They became quiet, and Mr Roland told Dick to come to him with his Maths book.

The tutor took it, and stretched his legs out under the table, leaning back to speak to Dick. To his enormous surprise his feet struck something soft and warm – and then something nipped him sharply on the ankle! He drew in his feet with a cry of pain.

The children stared at him. He bent down and looked under the table. 'It's that dog,' he said, in disgust. 'The brute snapped at my ankles. He has made a hole in my trousers. Take him out, Georgina.'

Georgina said nothing. She sat as though she had not heard.

'She won't answer if you call her Georgina,' Julian reminded him.

'She'll answer me whatever I call her,' said Mr Roland, in a low and angry voice. 'I won't have that dog in here. If you don't take him out this very minute, Georgina, I will go to your father.'

George looked at him. She knew perfectly well that if she didn't take Tim out, and Mr Roland went to her father, he would order Timothy to live in the garden kennel, and that would be dreadful. There was absolutely nothing to be done but obey. Red in the face, a huge frown almost hiding her eyes, she got up and spoke to Tim.

'Come on, Tim! I'm not surprised you bit him. I would, too, if I were a dog!'

'There is no need to be rude, Georgina,' said Mr Roland, angrily.

The others stared at George. They wondered how she dared to say things like that. When she got fierce it seemed as if she didn't care for anyone at all!

'Come back as soon as you have put the dog out,' said Mr Roland.

George scowled, but came back in a few minutes. She felt caught. Her father was friendly with Mr Roland, and knew how difficult George was – if she behaved as badly as she felt she would like to, it would be Tim who would suffer, for he would certainly be banished from the house. So for Tim's sake George obeyed the tutor – but from that moment she disliked him and resented him bitterly with all her fierce little heart.

The others were sorry for George and Timothy, but

they did not share the little girl's intense dislike of the new tutor. He often made them laugh. He was patient with their mistakes. He was willing to show them how to make paper darts and ships, and to do funny little tricks. Julian and Dick thought these were fun, and stored them up to try on the other boys when they went back to school.

After lessons that morning the children went out for half an hour in the frosty sunshine. George called Tim.

'Poor old boy!' she said. 'What a shame to turn you out of the room! Whatever did you snap at Mr Roland for? I think it was a very good idea, Tim – but I really don't know what made you!'

'George, you can't play about with Mr Roland,' said Julian. 'You'll only get into trouble. He's tough. He won't stand much from any of us. But I think he'll be quite a good sport if we get on the right side of him.'

'Well, get on the right side of him if you like,' said George, in rather a sneering voice. 'I'm not going to. If I don't like a person, I don't – and I don't like *him*.'

'Why? Just because he doesn't like Tim?' asked Dick.

'Mostly because of that – but because he makes me feel prickly down my back,' said George. 'I don't like his nasty mouth.'

'But you can't see it,' said Julian. 'It's covered with his moustache and beard.'

'I've seen his lips through them,' said George, obstinately. 'They're thin and cruel. You look and see. I don't like thin-lipped people. They are always spiteful and hard. And I don't like his cold eyes either. You can suck up to him all you like. *I* shan't.'

Julian refused to get angry with the stubborn little girl. He laughed at her. 'We're not going to suck up to him,' he said. 'We're just going to be sensible, that's all. You be sensible too, George, old thing.'

But once George had made up her mind about something nothing would alter her. She cheered up when she heard that they were all to go Christmas shopping on the bus that afternoon – without Mr Roland! He was going to watch an experiment that her father was going to show him.

'I will take you into the nearest town and you shall shop to your hearts' content,' said Aunt Fanny to the children. 'Then we will have tea in a tea-shop and catch the six o'clock bus home.'

This was fun. They caught the afternoon bus and rumbled along the deep country lanes till they got to the town. The shops looked very colourful and bright. The children had brought their money with them, and were very busy indeed, buying all kinds of things. There were so many people to get presents for!

'I suppose we'd better get something for Mr Roland, hadn't we?' said Julian.

'I'm going to,' said Anne.

'Fancy buying Mr *Roland* a present!' said George, in her scornful voice.

'Why shouldn't she, George?' asked her mother, in surprise. 'Oh dear, I hope you are going to be sensible about him, and not take a violent dislike to the poor man. I don't want him to complain to your father about you.'

'What are you going to buy for Tim, George?' asked Julian, changing the subject quickly.

'The largest bone the butcher has got,' said George. 'What are *you* going to buy him?'

'I guess if Tim had money, he would buy us each a present,' said Anne, taking hold of the thick hair round Tim's neck, and pulling it lovingly. 'He's the best dog in the world!'

George forgave Anne for saying she would buy Mr Roland a present, when the little girl said that about Tim! She cheered up again and began to plan what she would buy for everyone.

They had a fine tea, and caught the six o'clock bus back. Aunt Fanny went to see if the cook had given the two men their tea. She came out of the study beaming.

'Really, I've never seen your uncle so jolly,' she said to Julian and Dick. 'He and Mr Roland are getting on like a house on fire. He has been showing your tutor quite a lot of his experiments. It's nice for him to have someone to talk to that knows a little about these things.'

Mr Roland played games with the children that evening. Tim was in the room, and the tutor tried again to make friends with him, but the dog refused to take any notice of him.

'As sulky as his little mistress!' said the tutor, with a laughing look at George, who was watching Tim refuse to go to Mr Roland, and looking rather pleased about it. She gave the tutor a scowl and said nothing.

'Shall we ask him whether "VIA OCCULTA" really does mean "Secret Way" or not, tomorrow?' said Julian to Dick, as they undressed that night. 'I'm just longing to know if it does. What do you think of Mr Roland, Dick?'

'I don't really quite know,' said Dick. 'I like lots of things about him, but then I suddenly don't like him at all. I don't like his eyes. And George is quite right about his lips. They are so thin there's hardly anything of them at all.'

'I think he's all right,' said Julian. 'He won't stand any nonsense, that's all. I wouldn't mind showing him the whole piece of rag and asking him to make out its meaning for us.'

'I thought you said it was to be a proper secret,' said Dick.

'I know – but what's the use of a secret we don't know the meaning of ourselves?' said Julian. 'I'll tell you what we *could* do – ask him to explain the words to us, and not show him the bit of linen.'

'But we can't read some of the words ourselves,' said Dick. 'So that's no use. You'd have to show him the whole thing, and tell him where we got it.'

'Well, I'll see,' said Julian, getting into bed.

The next day there were lessons again from half-past nine to half-past twelve. George appeared without Tim. She was angry at having to do this, but it was no good being defiant and refusing to come to lessons without Tim. Now that he had snapped at Mr Roland, he had definitely put himself in the wrong, and the tutor had every right to refuse to allow him to come. But George looked very sulky indeed.

In the Latin lesson Julian took the chance of asking what he wanted to know. 'Please, Mr Roland,' he said, 'could you tell me what "VIA OCCULTA" means?'

'"VIA OCCULTA"' said Mr Roland, frowning. 'Yes – it means "Secret Path" or, "Secret Road". A hidden way – something like that. Why do you want to know?'

All the children were listening eagerly. Their hearts thumped with excitement. So Julian had been right. That funny bit of rag contained directions for some hidden way, some secret path – but where to! Where did it begin, and end?

'Oh – I just wanted to know,' said Julian. 'Thank you, sir.'

He winked at the others. He was as excited as they were. If only they could make out the rest of the markings, they might be able to solve the mystery. Well – perhaps he would ask Mr Roland in a day or two. The secret must be solved somehow.

'The "Secret Way",' said Julian to himself, as he worked out a problem in geometry. 'The "Secret Way". I'll find it somehow.'

7 Directions for the Secret Way

For the next day or two the four children did not really have much time to think about the Secret Way, because Christmas was coming near, and there was a good deal to do.

There were Christmas cards to draw and paint for their mothers and fathers and friends. There was the house to decorate. They went out with Mr Roland to find sprays of holly, and came home laden.

'You look like a Christmas card yourselves,' said Aunt Fanny, as they walked up the garden path, carrying the red-berried holly over their shoulders. Mr Roland had found a group of trees with tufts of mistletoe growing from the top branches, and they had brought some of that too. Its berries shone like pale green pearls.

'Mr Roland had to climb the tree to get this,' said Anne. 'He's a good climber – as good as a monkey.'

Everyone laughed except George. She never laughed at anything to do with the tutor. They all dumped their loads down in the porch, and went to wash. They were to decorate the house that evening.

'Is Uncle going to let his study be decorated too?' asked Anne. There were all kinds of strange instruments and glass tubes in the study now, and the children looked at them with wonder whenever they ventured into the study, which was very seldom.

'No, my study is certainly not to be messed about,'

said Uncle Quentin, at once. 'I wouldn't hear of it.'

'Uncle, why do you have all these funny things in your study?' asked Anne, looking round with wide eyes.

Uncle Quentin laughed. 'I'm looking for a secret formula!' he said.

'What's that?' said Anne.

'You wouldn't understand,' said her uncle. 'All these "funny things" as you call them, help me in my experiments, and I put down in my book what they tell me – and from all I learn I work out a secret formula, that will be of great use when it is finished.'

'You want to know a secret formula, and we want to know a secret way,' said Anne, quite forgetting that she was not supposed to talk about this.

Julian was standing by the door. He frowned at Anne. Luckily Uncle Quentin was not paying any more attention to the little girl's chatter. Julian pulled her out of the room.

'Anne, the only way to stop you giving away secrets is to sew up your mouth, like Brer Rabbit wanted to do to Mister Dog!' he said.

Joanna the cook was busy baking Christmas cakes. An enormous turkey had been sent over from Kirrin Farm, and was hanging up in the larder. Timothy thought it smelt glorious, and Joanna was always shooing him out of the kitchen.

There were boxes of crackers on the shelf in the sitting-room, and mysterious parcels everywhere. It was very, very Christmassy! The children were happy and excited.

Mr Roland went out and dug up a little spruce fir tree. 'We must have a Christmas tree,' he said. 'Have you any tree-ornaments, children?'

'No,' said Julian, seeing George shake her head.

'I'll go into the town this afternoon and get some for you,' promised the tutor. 'It will be fun dressing the tree. We'll put it in the hall, and light candles on it on Christmas Day after tea. Who's coming with me to get the candles and the ornaments?'

'I am!' cried three children. But the fourth said nothing. That was George. Not even to buy tree-ornaments would the obstinate little girl go with Mr Roland. She had never had a Christmas tree before, and she was very much looking forward to it – but it was spoilt for her because Mr Roland bought the things that made it so beautiful.

Now it stood in the hall, with coloured candles in holders clipped to the branches, and bright shining ornaments hanging from top to bottom. Silver strands of frosted string hung down from the branches like icicles, and Anne had put bits of white cotton-wool here and there to look like snow. It really was a lovely sight to see.

'Beautiful!' said Uncle Quentin, as he passed through the hall, and saw Mr Roland hanging the last ornaments on the tree. 'I say – look at the fairy doll on the top! Who's that for? A good girl?'

Anne secretly hoped that Mr Roland would give her the doll. She was sure it wasn't for George – and anyway, George wouldn't accept it. It was such a pretty doll, with its gauzy frock and silvery wings.

Julian, Dick and Anne had quite accepted the tutor now as teacher and friend. In fact, everyone had, their uncle and aunt too, and even Joanna the cook. George, of course, was the only exception, and she and Timothy kept away from Mr Roland, each looking as sulky as the other whenever the tutor was in the room.

'You know, I never knew a dog could look so

sulky!' said Julian, watching Timothy. 'Really, he scowls almost like George.'

'And I always feel as if George puts her tail down like Tim, when Mr Roland is in the room,' giggled Anne.

'Laugh all you like,' said George, in a low tone. 'I think you're beastly to me. I know I'm right about Mr Roland. I've got a feeling about him. And so has Tim.'

'You're silly, George,' said Dick. 'You haven't *really* got a Feeling – it's only that Mr Roland will keep calling you Georgina and putting you in your place, and that he doesn't like Tim. I dare say he can't help disliking dogs. After all, there was once a famous man called Lord Roberts who couldn't bear cats.'

'Oh well, cats are different,' said George. 'If a person doesn't like dogs, especially a dog like our Timothy, then there really *must* be something wrong with him.'

'It's no use arguing with George,' said Julian. 'Once she's made up her mind about something, she won't budge!'

George went out of the room in a huff. The others thought she was behaving rather stupidly.

'I'm surprised really,' said Anne. 'She was so jolly last term at school. Now she's gone all strange, rather like she was when we first knew her last summer.'

'I do think Mr Roland has been decent digging up the Christmas tree and everything,' said Dick. 'I still don't like him awfully much sometimes, but I think he's a sport. What about asking him if he can read that old linen rag for us – I don't think I'd mind him sharing our secret, really.'

'I would *love* him to share it,' said Anne, who was busy doing a marvellous Christmas card for the tutor. 'He's most awfully clever. I'm sure he could tell us what the Secret Way is. Do let's ask him.'

'All right,' said Julian. 'I'll show him the piece of linen. It's Christmas Eve tonight. He will be with us in the sitting-room, because Aunt Fanny is going into the study with Uncle Quentin to wrap up presents for all of us!'

So, that evening, before Mr Roland came in to sit with them, Julian took out the little roll of linen and stroked it out flat on the table. George looked at it in surprise.

'Mr Roland will be here in a minute,' she said. 'You'd better put it away quickly.'

'We're going to ask him if he can tell us what the old Latin words mean,' said Julian.

'You're not!' cried George, in dismay. 'Ask him to share our secret! How ever can you?'

'Well, we want to know what the secret is, don't we?' said Julian. 'We don't need to tell him where we got this or anything about it except that we want to know what the markings mean. We're not exactly sharing the secret with him – only asking him to use his brains to help us.'

'Well, I never thought you'd ask *him*,' said George. 'And he'll want to know simply everything about it, you just see if he won't! He's terribly snoopy.'

'Whatever do you mean?' said Julian, in surprise. 'I don't think he's a bit snoopy.'

'I saw him yesterday snooping round the study when no one was there,' said George. 'He didn't see me outside the window with Tim. He was having a real poke round.'

'You know how interested he is in your father's work,' said Julian. 'Why shouldn't he look at it? Your father likes him too. You're just seeing what horrid things you can find to say about Mr Roland.'

'Oh shut up, you two,' said Dick. 'It's Christmas Eve. Don't let's argue or quarrel or say beastly things.'

Just at that moment the tutor came into the room. 'All as busy as bees?' he said, his mouth smiling beneath its moustache. 'Too busy to have a game of cards, I suppose?'

'Mr Roland, sir,' began Julian, 'could you help us with something? We've got an old bit of linen here with odd markings on it. The words seem to be in some sort of Latin and we can't make them out.'

George gave an angry exclamation as she saw Julian push the piece of linen over towards the tutor. She went out of the room and shut the door with a bang. Tim was with her.

'Our sweet-tempered Georgina doesn't seem to be very friendly tonight,' remarked Mr Roland, pulling the bit of linen towards him. 'Where in the world did you get this? What an odd thing!'

Nobody answered. Mr Roland studied the roll of linen, and then gave an exclamation. 'Ah – I see why you wanted to know the meaning of those Latin words the other day – the ones that meant "hidden path", you remember. They are at the top of this linen roll.'

'Yes,' said Dick. All the children leaned over towards Mr Roland, hoping he would be able to unravel a little of the mystery for them.

'We just want to know the meaning of the words, sir,' said Julian.

'This is really very interesting,' said the tutor, puzzling over the linen. 'Apparently there are directions here for finding the opening or entrance of a secret path or road.'

'That's what we thought!' cried Julian, excitedly. 'That's exactly what we thought. Oh sir, do read the directions and see what you make of them.'

'Well, these eight squares are meant to represent wooden boards or panels, I think,' said the tutor, pointing to the eight rough squares drawn on the linen. 'Wait a minute – I can hardly read some of the words. This is most fascinating. *Solum lapideum – paries ligneus –* and what's this? – *cellula –* yes, *cellula!*'

The children hung on his words. 'Wooden panels!' That must mean panels somewhere at Kirrin Farmhouse.

Mr Roland frowned down at the old printed words. Then he sent Anne to borrow a magnifying glass from her uncle. She came back with it, and the four of them looked through the glass, seeing the words three times as clearly now.

'Well,' said the tutor at last, 'as far as I can make out the directions mean this: a room facing east; eight wooden panels, with an opening somewhere to be found in that marked one; a stone floor – yes, I think that's right, a stone floor, and a cupboard. It all sounds most extraordinary and very thrilling. Where *did* you get this from?'

'We just found it,' said Julian, after a pause. 'Oh Mr Roland, thanks awfully. We could never have made it out by ourselves. I suppose the entrance to the Secret Way is in a room facing east then.'

'It looks like it,' said Mr Roland, poring over the linen roll again. 'Where did you say you found this?'

'We didn't say,' said Dick. 'It's a secret really, you see.'

'I think you might tell me,' said the tutor, looking at Dick with his brilliant blue eyes. 'I can be trusted with secrets. You've no idea how many strange secrets I know.'

'Well,' said Julian, 'I don't really see why you shouldn't know where we found this, Mr Roland. We found it at Kirrin Farmhouse, in an old tobacco pouch. I suppose the Secret Way begins somewhere there! I wonder where and wherever can it lead to?'

'You found it at Kirrin Farmhouse!' exclaimed Mr Roland. 'Well, well – I must say that seems to be an interesting old place. I shall have to go over there one day.'

Julian rolled up the piece of linen and put it into his pocket. 'Well, thank you, sir,' he said. 'You've solved a bit of the mystery for us but set another puzzle! We must look for the entrance of the Secret Way after Christmas, when we can walk over to Kirrin Farmhouse.'

'I'll come with you,' said Mr Roland. 'I may be able to help a little. That is – if you don't mind me having a little share in this exciting secret.'

'Well – you've been such a help in telling us what the words mean,' said Julian, 'we'd like you to come if you want to, sir.'

'Yes, we *would*,' said Anne.

'We'll go and look for the Secret Way, then,' said Mr Roland. 'What fun we shall have, tapping round the panels, waiting for a mysterious dark entrance to appear!'

'I don't suppose George will go,' Dick murmured to Julian. 'You shouldn't have said Mr Roland could go with us, Ju. That means that old George will have to be left out of it. You know how she hates that.'

'I know,' said Julian, feeling uncomfortable. 'Don't let's worry about that now though. George may feel different after Christmas. She can't keep up this kind of behaviour for ever!'

8 What happened on Christmas night

It was great fun on Christmas morning. The children awoke early and tumbled out of bed to look at the presents that were stacked on chairs near-by. Squeals and yells of delight came from everyone.

'Oh! a railway station! Just what I wanted! Who gave me this marvellous station?'

'A new doll – with eyes that shut! I shall call her Betsy-May. She looks just like a Betsy-May!'

'I say – what a whopping great book – all about aeroplanes. From Aunt Fanny! How decent of her!'

'Timothy! Look what Julian has given you – a collar with big brass studs all round – you *will* be grand. Go and lick him to say thank you!'

'Who's this from? I say, who gave me this? Where's the label? Oh – from Mr Roland. How decent of him! Look, Julian, a pocket-knife with three blades!'

So the cries and exclamations went on, and the four excited children and the equally-excited dog spent a glorious hour before a late Christmas breakfast, opening all kinds and shapes of parcels. The bedrooms were in a fine mess when the children had finished!

'Who gave you that book about dogs, George?' asked Julian, seeing rather a nice dog-book lying on George's pile.

'Mr Roland,' said George, rather shortly. Julian

wondered if George was going to accept it. He rather thought she wouldn't. But the little girl, defiant and obstinate as she was, had made up her mind not to spoil Christmas Day by being 'difficult'. So, when the others thanked the tutor for their things she too added her thanks, though in rather a stiff little voice.

George had not given the tutor anything, but the others had, and Mr Roland thanked them all very heartily, appearing to be very pleased indeed. He told Anne that her Christmas card was the nicest he had ever had, and she beamed at him with joy.

'Well, I must say it's nice to be here for Christmas!' said Mr Roland, when he and the others were sitting round a loaded Christmas table, at the mid-day dinner. 'Shall I carve for you, Mr Quentin? I'm good at that!'

Uncle Quentin handed him the carving knife and fork gladly. 'It's nice to have you here,' he said warmly. 'I must say you've settled in well – I'm sure we all feel as if we've known you for ages!'

It really was a jolly Christmas Day. There were no lessons, of course, and there were to be none the next day either. The children gave themselves up to the enjoyment of eating a great deal, sucking sweets, and looking forward to the lighting of the Christmas tree.

It looked beautiful when the candles were lighted. They twinkled in the darkness of the hall, and the bright ornaments shone and glowed. Tim sat and looked at it, quite entranced.

'He likes it as much as we do,' said George. And indeed Tim had enjoyed the day just as much as any of them.

They were all tired out when they went to bed. 'I shan't be long before I'm asleep,' yawned Anne. 'Oh, George – it's been fun, hasn't it? I did like the Christmas tree.'

'Yes, it's been lovely,' said George, jumping into bed. 'Here comes Mother to say good-night. Basket, Tim, basket!'

Tim leapt into his basket by the window. He was always there when George's mother came into say good-night to the girls but as soon as she had gone downstairs, the dog took a flying leap and landed on George's bed. There he slept, his head curled round her feet.

'Don't you think Tim ought to sleep downstairs tonight?' said George's mother. 'Joanna says he ate such an enormous meal in the kitchen that she is sure he will be sick.'

'Oh *no*, Mother!' said George, at once. 'Make Tim sleep downstairs on Christmas night? Whatever would he think?'

'Oh, very well,' said her mother, with a laugh. 'I might have known it was useless to suggest it. Now to sleep quickly, Anne and George – it's late and you are all tired.'

She went into the boys' room and said good-night to them too. They were almost asleep.

Two hours later everyone else was in bed. The house was still and dark. George and Anne slept peacefully in their small beds. Timothy slept too, lying heavily on George's feet.

Suddenly George awoke with a jump. Tim was growling softly! He had raised his big shaggy head and George knew that he was listening.

'What is it, Tim?' she whispered. Anne did not wake. Tim went on growling softly. George sat up and put her hand on his collar to stop him. She knew that if he awoke her father, he would be cross.

Timothy stopped growling now that he had roused George. The girl sat and wondered what to do. It wasn't any good waking Anne. The little girl would be frightened. Why was Tim growling? He never did that at night!

'Perhaps I'd better go and see if everything is all right,' thought George. She was quite fearless, and the thought of creeping through the still, dark house did not disturb her at all. Besides she had Tim! Who could be afraid with Tim beside them!

She slipped on her dressing-gown. 'Perhaps a log has fallen out of one of the fire-places and a rug is burning,' she thought, sniffing as she went down the stairs. 'It would be just like Tim to smell it and warn us!'

With her hand on Tim's head to warn him to be quite quiet, George crept softly through the hall to the sitting-room. The fire was quite all right there, just a red glow. In the kitchen all was peace too. Tim's feet made a noise there, as his claws rattled against the linoleum.

A slight sound came from the other side of the house.

Tim growled quite loudly, and the hairs on the back of his neck rose up. George stood still. Could it possibly be burglars?

Suddenly Timothy shook himself free from her fingers and leapt across the hall, down a passage, and into the study beyond! There was the sound of an exclamation, and a noise as if someone was falling over.

'It *is* a burglar!' said George, and she ran to the study. She saw a torch shining on the floor, dropped by someone who was even now struggling with Tim.

George switched on the light, and then looked with the greatest astonishment into the study. Mr Roland was there in his dressing-gown, rolling on the floor, trying to get away from Timothy, who, although not biting him, was holding him firmly by his dressing-gown.

'Oh – it's you, George! Call your beastly dog off!' said Mr Roland, in a low and angry voice. 'Do you want to rouse all the household?'

'Why are you creeping about with a torch?' demanded George.

'I heard a noise down here, and came to see what it was,' said Mr Roland, sitting up and trying to fend off the angry dog. 'For goodness' sake, call your beast off.'

'Why didn't you put on the light?' asked George, not attempting to take Tim away. She was very much enjoying the sight of an angry and frightened Mr Roland.

'I couldn't find it,' said the tutor. 'It's on the wrong side of the door, as you see.'

This was true. The switch was an awkward one to find if you didn't know it. Mr Roland tried to push Tim away again, and the dog suddenly barked.

'Well – he'll wake everyone!' said the tutor, angrily. 'I didn't want to rouse the house. I thought I could find out for myself if there was anyone about – a burglar perhaps. Here comes your father!'

George's father appeared, carrying a large poker. He stood still in astonishment when he saw Mr Roland on the ground and Timothy standing over him.

'What's all this?' he exclaimed. Mr Roland tried to get up, but Tim would not let him. George's father called to him sternly.

'Tim! Come here, sir!'

Timothy glanced at George to see if his mistress agreed with her father's command. She said nothing. So Timothy took no notice of the order and merely made a snap at Mr Roland's ankles.

'That dog's mad!' said Mr Roland, from the floor. 'He's already bitten me once before, and now he's trying to do it again!'

'Tim! Will you come here, sir!' shouted George's father. 'George, that dog is really disobedient. Call him off at once.'

'Come here, Tim!' said George, in a low voice. The dog at once came to her, standing by her side with the hairs on his neck still rising up stiffly. He growled softly as if to say, 'Be careful, Mr Roland, be careful!'

The tutor got up. He was very angry indeed. He spoke to George's father.

'I heard some sort of noise and came down with my torch to see what it was,' he said. 'I thought it came from your study, and knowing you kept your valuable books and instruments here, I wondered if some thief was about. I had just got down, and into the room, when that dog appeared from somewhere and got me down on the ground! George came along too, and would not call him off.'

'I can't understand your behaviour, George; I really can't,' said her father, angrily. 'I hope you are not going to behave stupidly, as you used to behave before your cousins came last summer. And what is this I hear about Tim biting Mr Roland before?'

'George had him under the table during lessons,' said Mr Roland. 'I didn't know that, and when I stretched out my legs, they touched Tim, and he bit me. I didn't tell you before, sir, because I didn't want to trouble you. Both George and the dog have tried to annoy me ever since I have been here.'

'Well, Tim must go outside and live in the kennel,' said George's father. 'I won't have him in the house. It will be a punishment for him, and a punishment for you too, George. I will not have this kind of behaviour. Mr Roland has been extremely kind to you all.'

'I won't let Tim live outside,' said George furiously. 'It's such cold weather, and it would simply break his heart.'

'Well, his heart must be broken then,' said her father. 'It will depend entirely on your behaviour from now on whether Tim is allowed in the house at all these holidays. I shall ask Mr Roland each day how you have behaved. If you have a bad report, then Tim stays outside. Now you know! Go back to bed but first apologise to Mr Roland!'

'I won't!' said George, and choked by feelings of anger and dismay, she tore out of the room and up the stairs. The two men stared after her.

'Let her be,' said Mr Roland. 'She's a very difficult child – and has made up her mind not to like me, that's quite plain. But I shall be very glad to know that that dog isn't in the house. I'm not at all certain that Georgina wouldn't set him on me, if she could!'

'I'm sorry about all this,' said George's father. 'I wonder what the noise was that you heard? – a log falling in the grate I expect. Now – what am I to do about that tiresome dog tonight? Go and take him outside, I suppose!'

'Leave him tonight,' said Mr Roland. 'I can hear noises upstairs – the others are awake by now! Don't let's make any more disturbance tonight.'

'Perhaps you are right,' said George's father, thankfully. He didn't at all want to tackle a defiant little girl and an angry big dog in the middle of a cold night!

The two men went to bed and slept. George did not sleep. The others had been awake when she got upstairs, and she had told them what had happened.

'George! You really are an idiot!' said Dick. 'After all, why shouldn't Mr Roland go down if he heard a noise! *You* went down! Now we shan't have darling old Tim in the house this cold weather!'

Anne began to cry. She didn't like hearing that the tutor she liked so much had been knocked down by Tim, and she hated hearing that Tim was to be punished.

'Don't be a baby,' said George. '*I'm* not crying, and it's *my* dog!'

But, when everyone had settled down again in bed, and slept peacefully, George's pillow was very wet indeed. Tim crept up beside her and licked the salt tears off her cheek. He whined softly. Tim was always unhappy when his little mistress was sad.

9 A hunt for the Secret Way

There were no lessons the next day. George looked rather pale, and was very quiet. Tim was already out in the yard-kennel, and the children could hear him whining unhappily. They were all upset to hear him.

'Oh, George, I'm awfully sorry about it all,' said Dick. 'I wish you wouldn't get so fierce about things. You only get yourself into trouble – and poor old Tim.'

George was full of mixed feelings. She disliked Mr Roland so much now that she could hardly bear to look at him – and yet she did not dare to be openly rude and rebellious because she was afraid that if she was, the tutor would give her a bad report, and perhaps she would not be allowed even to *see* Timothy. It was very hard for a defiant nature like hers to force herself to behave properly.

Mr Roland took no notice of her at all. The other children tried to bring George into their talks and plans, but she remained quiet and uninterested.

'George! We're going over to Kirrin Farmhouse today,' said Dick. 'Coming? We're going to try and find the entrance to the Secret Way. It must start somewhere there.'

The children had told George what Mr Roland had said about the piece of marked linen. They had all been thrilled about this, though the excitements of

Christmas Day had made them forget about it for a while.

'Yes – of course I'll come,' said George, looking more cheerful. 'Timothy can come too. He wants a walk.'

But when the little girl found that Mr Roland was also going, she changed her mind at once. Not for anything would she go with the tutor! No – she would go for a walk alone with Timothy.

'But, George, think of the excitement we'll have trying to find the Secret Way,' said Julian, taking hold of her arm. George wrenched it away.

'I'm not going if Mr Roland is,' she said, obstinately, and the others knew that it was no good trying to coax her.

'I shall go alone with Tim,' said George. 'You go off together with your dear Mr Roland!'

She set out with Timothy, a lonely little figure going down the garden path. The others stared after her. This was horrid. George was being more and more left out, but what could they do about it?

'Well, children, are you ready?' asked Mr Roland. 'You start off by yourselves, will you? I'll meet you at the farmhouse later. I want to run down to the village first to get something.'

So the three children set off by themselves. wishing that George was with them. She was nowhere to be seen.

Old Mr and Mrs Sanders were pleased to see the three children, and sat them down in the big kitchen to eat ginger buns and drink hot milk.

'Well, have you come to find a few more secret things?' asked Mrs Sanders, with a smile.

'May we try?' asked Julian. 'We're looking for

a room that's facing east, with a stone floor, and panelling!'

'All the rooms downstairs have stone floors,' said Mrs Sanders. 'You hunt all you like, my dears. You won't do any damage, I know. But don't go into the room upstairs with the cupboard that has a false back, will you, or the one next to it! Those are the rooms the two artists have.'

'All right,' said Julian, rather sorry that they were unable to fiddle about with the exciting cupboard again. 'Are the artists here, Mrs Sanders? I'd like to talk to them about pictures. I hope one day I'll be an artist too.'

'Dear me, is that so?' said Mrs Sanders. 'Well, well – it's always a marvel to me how people make any money at painting pictures.'

'It isn't making money that artists like, so much as the painting of the pictures,' said Julian, looking rather wise. That seemed to puzzle Mrs Sanders even more. She shook her head and laughed.

'They're peculiar folk!' she said. 'Ah well – you go along and have a hunt for whatever it is you want to find. You can't talk to the two artists today though, Master Julian – they're out.'

The children finished their buns and milk and then stood up, wondering where to begin their search. They must look for a room or rooms facing east. That would be the first thing to do.

'Which side of the house faces east, Mrs Sanders?' asked Julian. 'Do you know?'

'The kitchen faces due north,' said Mrs Sanders. 'So east will be over there,' she pointed to the left.

'Thanks,' said Julian. 'Come on, everyone!' The three children went out of the kitchen, and turned to the left. There were three rooms there – a kind of scullery, not much used now, a tiny room used as a den by old Mr Sanders, and a room that had once been a drawing-room, but which was now cold and unused.

'They've all got stone floors,' said Julian.

'So we'll have to hunt through all of the three rooms,' said Anne.

'No, we won't,' said Julian. 'We shan't have to look in this scullery, for one thing!'

'Why not?' asked Anne.

'Because the walls are of stone, silly, and we want panelling,' said Julian. 'Use your brains, Anne!'

'Well, that's one room we needn't bother with, then,' said Dick. 'Look – both this little room and the drawing-room have panelling, Julian. We must search in both.'

'There must be some reason for putting *eight* squares of panelling in the directions,' said Julian, looking at the roll of linen again. 'It would be a good idea to see whether there's a place with eight squares only – you know, over a window, or something.'

It was tremendously exciting to look round the two rooms! The children began with the smaller room. It was panelled all the way round in dark oak, but there was no place where only eight panels showed. So the children went into the next room.

The panelling there was different. It did not look so old, and was not so dark. The squares were rather a different size, too. The children tried each panel, tapping and pressing as they went, expecting at any moment to see one slide back as the one in the hall had done.

But they were disappointed. Nothing happened at all. They were still in the middle of trying when they heard footsteps in the hall, and voices. Somebody looked into the drawing-room. It was a man, thin and tall, wearing glasses on his long nose.

'Hallo!' he said. 'Mrs Sanders told me you were treasure-hunting, or something. How are you getting on?'

'Not very well,' said Julian, politely. He looked at the man, and saw behind him another one, younger, with rather screwed-up eyes and a big mouth. 'I suppose you are the two artists?' he asked.

'We are!' said the first man, coming into the room. 'Now, just exactly what are you looking for?'

Julian did not really want to tell him, but it was difficult not to. 'Well – we're just seeing if there's a sliding panel here,' he said at last. 'There's one in the hall, you know. It's exciting to hunt round.'

'Shall we help?' said the first artist, coming into the room. 'What are your names? Mine's Thomas, and my friend's name is Wilton.'

The children talked politely for a minute or two, not at all wanting the two men to help. If there was anything to be found, *they* wanted to find it. It would spoil everything if grown-ups solved the puzzle!

Soon everyone was tap-tap-tapping round the wooden panels. They were in the middle of this when a voice hailed them.

'Hallo! My word, we *are* all busy!'

The children turned, and saw their tutor standing in the doorway, smiling at them. The two artists looked at him.

'Is this a friend of yours?' asked Mr Thomas.

'Yes – he's our tutor, and he's very nice!' said Anne, running to Mr Roland and putting her hand in his.

'Perhaps you will introduce me, Anne,' said Mr Roland, smiling at the little girl.

Anne knew how to introduce people. She had often seen her mother doing it. 'This is Mr Roland,' she said to the two artists. Then she turned to Mr Roland. 'This is Mr Thomas,' she said, waving her hand towards him, 'and the other one is Mr Wilton.'

The men half-bowed to one another and nodded. 'Are you staying here?' asked Mr Roland. 'A very nice old farmhouse, isn't it?'

'It isn't time to go yet, is it?' asked Julian, hearing a clock strike.

'Yes, I'm afraid it is,' said Mr Roland. 'I'm later meeting you than I expected. We must go in about five minutes – no later. I'll just give you a hand in trying to find this mysterious secret way!'

But no matter how any one of them pressed and tapped around the panels in either of the two rooms, they could not find anything exciting. It really was most disappointing.

'Well, we really must go now,' said Mr Roland. 'Come and say good-bye to Mrs Sanders.'

They all went into the warm kitchen, where Mrs Sanders was cooking something that smelt most delicious.

'Something for our lunch, Mrs Sanders?' said Mr Wilton. 'My word, you really are a wonderful cook!'

Mrs Sanders smiled. She turned to the children. 'Well, dearies, did you find what you wanted?' she asked.

'No,' said Mr Roland, answering for them. 'We haven't been able to find the secret way, after all!'

'The secret way?' said Mrs Sanders, in surprise. 'What do you know about that now? I thought it had all been forgotten – in fact, I haven't believed in that secret way for many a year!'

'Oh, Mrs Sanders – do you know about it?' cried Julian. 'Where is it?'

'I don't know, dear – the secret of it has been lost for

many a day,' said the old lady. 'I remember my old grandmother telling me something about it when I was smaller than any of you. But I wasn't interested in things like that when I was little. I was all for cows and hens and sheep.'

'Oh, Mrs Sanders – do, do try and remember something!' begged Dick. 'What *was* the secret way?'

'Well, it was supposed to be a hidden way from Kirrin Farmhouse to somewhere else,' said Mrs Sanders. 'I don't know where, I'm sure. It was used in the olden days when people wanted to hide from enemies.'

It was disappointing that Mrs Sanders knew so little. The children said good-bye and went off with their tutor, feeling that their morning had been wasted.

George was indoors when they got to Kirrin Cottage. Her cheeks were not so pale, now, and she greeted the children eagerly.

'Did you discover anything? Tell me all about it!' she said.

'There's nothing to tell,' said Dick, rather gloomily. 'We found three rooms facing east, with stone floors, but only two of them had wooden panelling, so we hunted round those, tapping and punching – but there wasn't anything to be discovered at all.'

'We saw the two artists,' said Anne. 'One was tall and thin and had a long nose with glasses on. He was called Mr Thomas. The other was younger, with little piggy eyes and an enormous mouth.'

'I met them out this morning,' said George. 'It must have been them. Mr Roland was with them, and they were all talking together. They didn't see me.'

'Oh, it couldn't have been the artists you saw,' said Anne, at once. 'Mr Roland didn't know them, I had to introduce them.'

'Well, I'm sure I heard Mr Roland call one of them Wilton,' said George, puzzled. 'He *must* have known them.'

'It couldn't have been the artists,' said Anne, again. 'They really didn't know Mr Roland. Mr Thomas asked if he was a friend of ours.'

'I'm sure I'm not mistaken,' said George, looking obstinate. 'If Mr Roland said he didn't know the two artists, he was telling lies.'

'Oh, you're always making out that he is doing something horrid!' cried Anne, indignantly. 'You just make up things about him!'

'Sh!' said Julian. 'Here he is.'

The door opened and the tutor came in. 'Well,' he said, 'it *was* disappointing that we couldn't find the secret way, wasn't it? Anyway, we were rather foolish to hunt about that drawing-room as we did – the panelling there wasn't really old – it must have been put in years after the other.'

'Oh – well, it's no good looking there again,' said Julian, disappointed. 'And I'm pretty sure there's nothing to be found in that other little room. We went all over it so thoroughly. Isn't it disappointing?'

'It is,' said Mr Roland. 'Well, Julian, how did you like the two artists? I was pleased to meet them – they seemed nice fellows, and I shall like to know them.'

George looked at the tutor. Could he possibly be telling untruths in such a truthful voice? The little girl was very puzzled. She felt sure it was the artists she had seen him with. But why should he pretend he didn't know them? She must be mistaken. But all the same, she felt uncomfortable about it, and made up her mind to find out the truth, if she could.

10   A shock for George and Tim

Next morning there were lessons again – and no Timothy under the table! George felt very much inclined to refuse to work, but what would be the good of that? Grown-ups were so powerful, and could dole out all kinds of punishments. She didn't care how much she was punished herself but she couldn't bear to think that Timothy might have to share in the punishments too.

So, pale and sullen, the little girl sat down at the table with the others. Anne was eager to join in the lessons – in fact she was eager to do anything to please Mr Roland, because he had given her the fairy doll from the top of the Christmas tree! Anne thought it was the prettiest doll she had ever seen.

George had scowled at the doll when Anne showed it to her. She didn't like dolls, and she certainly wasn't going to like one that Mr Roland had chosen, and given to Anne! But Anne loved it, and had made up her mind to do lessons with the others, and work as well as she could.

George did as little as she could without getting into trouble. Mr Roland took no interest in her or in her work. He praised the others, and took a lot of trouble to show Julian something he found difficult.

The children heard Tim whining outside as they worked. This troubled them very much, for Timothy was such a companion, and so dear to them all. They could not bear to think of him left out of everything, cold and miserable in the yard-kennel. When the ten minutes' break came, and Mr Roland went out of the room for a few minutes, Julian spoke to George.

'George! It's awful for us to hear poor old Tim whining out there in the cold. And I'm sure I heard him cough. Let me speak to Mr Roland about him. You must feel simply dreadful knowing that Tim is out there.'

'I thought I heard him cough, too,' said George, looking worried. 'I hope he won't get a cold. He simply doesn't understand why I have to put him there. He thinks I'm terribly unkind.'

The little girl turned her head away, afraid that tears might come into her eyes. She always boasted that she never cried – but it was very difficult to keep the tears away when she thought of Timothy out there in the cold.

Dick took her arm. 'Listen, George – you just hate Mr Roland, and I suppose you can't help it. But we can none of us bear Timothy being out there all alone – and it looks like snow today, which would be awful for him. Could you be awfully, awfully good today, and forget your dislike, so that when your father asks Mr Roland for your report, he can say you were very good – and then we'll ask Mr Roland if he wouldn't let Timmy come back into the house.'

'See?'

Timothy coughed again, out in the yard, and George's heart went cold. Suppose he got that awful illness called pneumonia – and she couldn't nurse him because he had to live in the kennel? She would die of unhappiness! She turned to Julian and Dick.

'All right,' she said. 'I do hate Mr Roland – but I love Timothy more than I hate the tutor – so for Tim's sake

I'll pretend to be good and sweet and hard-working. And then you can beg him to let Timothy come back.'

'Good girl!' said Julian. 'Now here he comes – so do your best.'

To the tutor's enormous surprise, George gave him a smile when he came into the room. This was so unexpected that it puzzled him. He was even more puzzled to find that George worked harder than anyone for the rest of the morning, and she answered politely and cheerfully when he spoke to her. He gave her a word of praise.

'Well done, Georgina! I can see you've got brains.'

'Thank you,' said George, and gave him another wan smile – a very watery, poor affair, compared with the happy smiles the others had been used to – but still, it *was* a smile!

At dinner-time George looked after Mr Roland most politely – passed him the salt, offered him more bread, got up to fill his glass when it was empty! The others looked at her in admiration. George had plenty of pluck. She must be finding it very difficult to behave as if Mr Roland was a great friend, when she really disliked him so much!

Mr Roland seemed very pleased, and appeared to be quite willing to respond to George's friendliness. He made a little joke with her, and offered to lend her a book he had about a dog. George's mother was delighted to find that her difficult daughter seemed to be turning over a new leaf. Altogether things were very much happier that day.

'George, you go out of the room before your father comes in to ask Mr Roland about your behaviour tonight,' said Julian. 'Then, when the tutor gives you a splendid report, we will all ask if Timothy can come back. It will be easier if you are not there.'

'All right,' said George. She was longing for this difficult day to be over. It was very hard for her to pretend to be friendly, when she was not. She could never never do it, if it wasn't for Timothy's sake!

George disappeared out of the room just before six o'clock, when she heard her father coming. He walked into the room and nodded to Mr Roland.

'Well? Have your pupils worked well today?' he asked.

'Very well indeed,' said Mr Roland. 'Julian has really mastered something he didn't understand today. Dick has done well in Latin. Anne has written out a French exercise without a single mistake!'

'And what about George?' asked Uncle Quentin.

'I was coming to Georgina,' said Mr Roland, looking round and seeing that she was gone. 'She has worked better than anyone else today! I am really pleased with her. She has tried hard – and she has really been polite and friendly. I feel she is trying to turn over a new leaf.'

'She's been a brick today,' said Julian, warmly. 'Uncle Quentin, she has tried awfully hard, she really has. And, you know, she's terribly unhappy.'

'Why?' asked Uncle Quentin in surprise.

'Because of Timothy,' said Julian. 'He's out in the cold, you see. And he's got a dreadful cough.'

'Oh, Uncle Quentin, please do let poor Timmy come indoors,' begged Anne.

'Yes, please do,' said Dick. 'Not only for George's sake, because she loves him so, but for us too. We hate to hear him whining outside. And George does deserve a reward, Uncle – she's been marvellous today.'

'Well,' said Uncle Quentin, looking doubtfully at the three eager faces before him, 'well – I hardly know what to say. If George is going to be sensible – and the weather gets colder – well . . .'

He looked at Mr Roland, expecting to hear him say something in favour of Timothy. But the tutor said nothing. He looked annoyed.

'What do you think, Mr Roland?' asked Uncle Quentin.

'I think you should keep to what you said and let the dog stay outside,' said the tutor. 'George is spoilt, and needs firm handling. You should really keep to your decision about the dog. There is no reason to give way about it just because she tried to be good for once!'

The three children stared at Mr Roland in surprise and dismay. It had never entered their heads that he would not back them up!

'Oh, Mr Roland, you *are* horrid!' cried Anne. 'Oh do, do say you'll have Timothy back.'

The tutor did not look at Anne. He pursed up his mouth beneath its thick moustache and looked straight at Uncle Quentin.

'Well,' said Uncle Quentin, 'perhaps we had better see how George behaves for a whole week. After all – just one day isn't much.'

The children stared at him in disgust. They thought he was weak and unkind. Mr Roland nodded his head.

'Yes,' he said, 'a week will be a better test. If Georgina behaves well for a whole week, we'll have another word about the dog. But at present I feel it would be better to keep him outside.'

'Very well,' said Uncle Quentin, and went out of the room. He paused to look back. 'Come along into my study sometime,' he said. 'I've got a bit further with my formula. It's at a very interesting stage.'

The three children looked at one another but said nothing. How mean of the tutor to stop Uncle

Quentin from having Timothy indoors again! They all felt disappointed in him. The tutor saw their faces.

'I'm sorry to disappoint you,' he said. 'But I think if you'd been bitten by Timothy once and snapped at all over when he got you on the floor, you would not be very keen on having him in either!'

He went out of the room. The children wondered what to say to George. She came in a moment later, her face eager. But when she saw the gloomy looks of the other three, she stopped short.

'Isn't Tim to come in?' she asked, quickly. 'What's happened? Tell me!'

They told her. The little girl's face grew dark and angry when she heard how the tutor had put his foot down about Timothy, even when her father had himself suggested that the dog might come indoors.

'Oh, what a beast he is!' she cried. 'How I do hate him! I'll pay him back for this. I will, I will, I will!'

She rushed out of the room. They heard her fumbling in the hall, and then the front door banged.

'She's gone out into the dark,' said Julian. 'I bet she's gone to Timmy. Poor old George. Now she'll be worse than ever!'

That night George could not sleep. She lay and tossed in her bed, listening for Timothy. She heard him cough. She heard him whine. He was cold, she knew he was. She had put plenty of fresh straw into his kennel and had turned it away from the cold north wind – but he must feel the bitter night terribly, after sleeping for so long on her bed!

Timothy gave such a hollow cough that George could bear it no longer. She must, she simply must, get up and go down to him. 'I shall bring him into the house for a little while and rub his chest with some of that stuff Mother uses for herself when she's got a cold

on her chest,' thought the girl. 'Perhaps that will do
him good.'

She quickly put a few clothes on and crept downstairs. The whole house was quiet. She slipped out into
the yard and undid Tim's chain. He was delighted to
see her and licked her hands and face lovingly.

'Come along into the warm for a little while,'
whispered the little girl. 'I'll rub your poor chest with
some oil I've got.'

Timmy pattered behind her into the house. She took
him to the kitchen – but the fire was out and the room
was cold. George went to look at the other rooms.

There was quite a nice fire still in her father's study.
She and Tim went in there. She did not put on the
light, because the firelight was fairly bright. She had
with her the little bottle of oil from the bathroom
cupboard. She put it down by the fire to warm.

Then she rubbed the dog's hairy chest with the oil,
hoping it would do him good. 'Don't cough now if
you can help it, Tim,' she whispered. 'If you do,
someone may hear you. Lie down here by the fire,
darling, and get nice and warm. Your cold will soon be
better.'

Timothy lay down on the rug. He was glad to be out
of his kennel and with his beloved mistress. He put his
head on her knee. She stroked him and whispered to
him.

The firelight glinted on the curious instruments and
glass tubes that stood around on shelves in her father's
study. A log shifted a little in the fire and settled lower,
sending up a cloud of sparks. It was warm and peaceful
there.

The little girl almost fell asleep. The big dog closed
his eyes too, and rested peacefully, happy and warm.
George settled down with her head on his neck.

She awoke to hear the study clock striking six! The room was cold now, and she shivered. Goodness! Six o'clock! Joanna the cook would soon be awake. She must not find Timmy and George in the study!

'Tim darling! Wake up! We must put you back into your kennel,' whispered George. 'I'm sure your cold is better, because you haven't coughed once since you've been indoors. Get up – and don't make a noise. Sh!'

Tim stood up and shook himself. He licked George's hand. He understood perfectly that he must be quite quiet. The two of them slipped out of the study, went into the hall and out of the front door.

In a minute or two Timothy was on the chain, and in his kennel, cuddled down among the straw. George wished she could cuddle there with him. She gave him a pat and slipped back indoors again.

She went up to bed, sleepy and cold. She forgot that she was partly dressed and got into bed just as she was. She was asleep in a moment!

In the morning Anne was most amazed to find that George had on vest, knickers, jeans and jersey, when she got out of bed to dress.

'Look!' she said. 'You're half-dressed! But I *saw* you undressing last night.'

'Be quiet,' said George. 'I went down and let Tim in last night. We sat in front of the study fire and I rubbed him with oil. Now don't you dare to say a word to anyone! Promise!'

Anne promised – and she faithfully kept her word. Well, well – to think that George dared to roam about like that all night – what an extraordinary girl she was!

11 Stolen papers

'George, don't behave fiercely today, will you?' said Julian, after breakfast. 'It won't do you or Timothy any good at all.'

'Do you suppose I'm going to behave well when I know perfectly well that Mr Roland will never let me have Tim indoors all these holidays?' said George.

'Well – they said a week,' said Dick. 'Can't you try for a week?'

'No. At the end of a week Mr Roland will say I must try for another week,' said George. 'He's got a real dislike for poor Tim. And for me too. I'm not surprised at that, because I know that when I try to be horrid, I really *am* horrid. But he shouldn't hate poor Timmy.'

'Oh George – you'll spoil the whole hols if you are silly, and keep getting into trouble,' said Anne.

'Well, I'll spoil them then,' said George, the sulky look coming back on her face.

'I don't see why you have to spoil them for *us*, as well as for yourself,' said Julian.

'They don't need to be spoilt for you,' said George. 'You can have all the fun you want – go for walks with your dear Mr Roland, play games with him in the evening, and laugh and talk as much as you like. You don't need to take any notice of me.'

'You are a funny girl, George,' said Julian, with a sigh. 'We like you, and we hate you to be unhappy – so

how can we have fun if we know you're miserable –
and Timmy too?'

'Don't worry about *me*,' said George, in rather a
choky voice. 'I'm going out to Tim. I'm not coming in
to lessons today.'

'George! But you must!' said Dick and Julian
together.

'There's no "must" about it,' said George. 'I'm just
not coming. I won't work with Mr Roland till he says I
can have Timothy indoors again.'

'But you know you can't do things like that – you'll
be told off or something,' said Dick.

'I shall run away if things get too bad,' said George,
in a shaky voice. 'I shall run away with Tim.'

She went out of the room and shut the door with a
bang. The others stared after her. What could you do
with a person like George? Anyone could rule her with
kindness and understanding – but as soon as she came
up against anyone who disliked her, or whom she
disliked, she shied away like a frightened horse – and
kicked like a frightened horse, too!

Mr Roland came into the sitting-room, his books in
his hand. He smiled at the three children.

'Well? All ready for me, I see. Where's Georgina?'

Nobody answered. Nobody was going to give
George away!

'Don't you know where she is?' asked Mr Roland in
surprise. He looked at Julian.

'No, sir,' said Julian, truthfully. 'I've no idea where
she is.'

'Well – perhaps she will come along in a few
minutes,' said Mr Roland. 'Gone to feed that dog of
hers, I suppose.'

They all settled down to work. The time went on
and George did not come in. Mr Roland glanced at the

clock and made an impatient clicking noise with his tongue.

'Really, it's too bad of Georgina to be so late! Anne, go and see if you can find her.'

Anne went. She looked in the bedroom. There was no George there. She looked in the kitchen. Joanna was there, making cakes. She gave the little girl a hot piece to eat. She had no idea where George was.

Anne couldn't find her anywhere. She went back and told Mr Roland. He looked angry.

'I shall have to report this to her father,' he said. 'I have never had to deal with such a rebellious child before. She seems to do everything she possibly can to get herself into trouble.'

Lessons went on. Break came, and still George did not appear. Julian slipped out and saw that the yard-kennel was empty. So George had gone out with Timmy! What a row she would get into when she got back!

No sooner had the children settled down after break to do the rest of the morning's lessons, than a big disturbance came.

Uncle Quentin burst in looking upset and worried.

'Have any of you children been into my study?' he asked.

'No, Uncle Quentin,' they all answered.

'You said we weren't to,' said Julian.

'Why?' Has something been broken?' asked Mr Roland.

'Yes – the test-tubes I set yesterday for an experiment have been broken – and what is worse, three most important pages of my book have gone,' said Uncle Quentin. 'I can write them out again, but only after a great deal of work. I can't understand it. Are you *sure*, children, that none of you has been meddling with things in my study?'

'Quite sure,' they answered. Anne went very red – she suddenly remembered what George had told her. George said she had taken Timmy into Uncle Quentin's study last night, and rubbed his chest with oil! But George couldn't possibly have broken the test-tubes, and taken pages from her father's book!

Mr Roland noticed that Anne had gone red.

'Do you know anything about this, Anne?' he asked.

'No, Mr Roland,' said Anne, blushing even redder, and looking very uncomfortable indeed.

'Where's George?' suddenly said Uncle Quentin.

The children said nothing, and it was Mr Roland who answered:

'We don't know. She didn't come to lessons this morning.'

'Didn't come to lessons! Why not?' demanded Uncle Quentin, beginning to frown.

'She didn't say,' said Mr Roland dryly. 'I imagine she was upset because we were firm about Timothy last night, and this is her way of being defiant.'

'The naughty girl!' said George's father, angrily. 'I don't know what's come over her lately. Fanny! Come here! Did you know that George hasn't been in to her lessons today?'

Aunt Fanny came into the room. She looked very worried. She had a little bottle in her hand. The children wondered what it was.

'Didn't come in to lessons!' repeated Aunt Fanny. 'How extraordinary! Then where is she?'

'I don't think you need to worry about her,' said Mr Roland, smoothly. 'She's probably gone off with Timothy in a fit of temper. What is very much more important, is the fact that your work appears to have been spoilt by someone. I only hope it is not George, who has been spiteful enough to get back at you for not allowing her to have her dog in the house.'

'Of *course* it wasn't George!' cried Dick, angry that anyone should even think such a thing of his cousin.

'George would never, never do a thing like that,' said Julian.

'No, she never would,' said Anne, sticking up valiantly for her cousin, although a horrid doubt was in her mind. After all – George *had* been in the study last night!

'Quentin, I am sure George would not even *think* of such a thing,' said Aunt Fanny. 'You will find those pages somewhere – and as for the test-tubes that were broken, well, perhaps the wind blew the curtain against them, or something! When did you last see those pages?'

'Last night,' said Uncle Quentin. 'I read them over again, and checked my figures to make sure they were right. Those pages contain the very heart of my formula! If they got into anyone else's hands, they could use my secret. This is a terrible thing for me! I *must* know what has happened to them.'

'I found this in your study, Quentin,' said Aunt Fanny, and she held up the little bottle she carried. 'Did you put it there? It was in the fender.'

Uncle Quentin took the bottle and stared at it. 'Camphorated oil!' he said. 'Of course I didn't take it there. Why should I?'

'Well – who took it there, then?' asked Aunt Fanny, puzzled. 'None of the children has a cold – and anyway, they wouldn't think of the camphorated oil, and take it into the study to use! It's most extraordinary!'

Everyone was astonished. Why should a bottle of

camphorated oil appear in the study fender?

Only one person could think why. It suddenly came into Anne's mind in a flash. George had said she had taken Timmy into the study, and rubbed him with oil! He had had a cough, that was why. And she had left the oil in the study. Oh dear, oh dear – now what would happen? What a pity George had forgotten the oil!

Anne went very red again as she looked at the oil. Mr Roland, whose eyes seemed very sharp this morning, looked hard at the little girl.

'Anne! You know something about that oil!' he said suddenly. 'What do you know? Did you put it there?'

'No,' said Anne. 'I haven't been into the study. I said I hadn't.'

'Do you know anything about the oil?' said Mr Roland, again. 'You *do* know something.'

Everyone stared at Anne. She stared back. This was simply dreadful. She could not give George away. She could *not*. George was in quite enough trouble as it was, without getting into any more. She pursed up her little mouth and did not answer.

'Anne!' said Mr Roland, sternly. 'Answer when you are spoken to.'

Anne said nothing. The two boys stared at her, guessing that it was something to do with George. They did not know that George had brought Timothy in the night before.

'Anne, dear,' said her aunt, gently. 'Tell us if you know something. It might help us to find out what has happened to Uncle Quentin's papers. It is very, very, important.'

Still Anne said nothing. Her eyes filled with tears. Julian squeezed her arm.

'Don't bother Anne,' he said to the grown-ups. 'If

she thinks she can't tell you, she's got some very good reason.'

'I think she's shielding George,' said Mr Roland. 'Is that it, Anne?'

Anne burst into tears. Julian put his arms round his little sister, and spoke again to the three grown-ups.

'*Don't* bother Anne! Can't you see she's upset?'

'We'll let George speak for herself, when she thinks she will come in,' said Mr Roland. 'I'm sure she knows how that bottle got there – and if she put it there herself she must have been into the study – and she's the only person that *has* been there.'

The boys could not think for one moment that George would do such a thing as spoil her father's work. Anne feared it, and it upset her. She sobbed in Julian's arms.

'When George comes in, send her to me in my study,' said Uncle Quentin, irritably. 'How can a man work when these upsets go on? I was always against having children in the house.'

He stamped out, tall, cross and frowning. The children were glad to see him go. Mr Roland shut the books on the table with a snap.

'We can't do any more lessons this morning,' he said. 'Put on your things and go out for a walk till dinner-time.'

'Yes, do,' said Aunt Fanny, looking white and worried. 'That's a good idea.'

Mr Roland and their aunt went out of the room. 'I don't know if Mr Roland thinks he's coming out with us,' said Julian, in a low voice, 'but we've got to get out first and give him the slip. We've got to find George and warn her what's up.'

'Right!' said Dick. 'Dry your eyes, Anne darling. Hurry and get your things. We'll slip out of the garden door before Mr Roland comes down. I bet George has gone for her favourite walk over the cliffs. We'll meet her!' The three children threw on their outdoor things and crept out of the garden door quietly. They raced down the garden path, and out of the gate before Mr Roland even knew they were gone! They made their way to the cliffs, and looked to see if George was coming.

'There she is – and Timothy, too!' cried Julian, pointing. 'George! George! Quick, we've got something to tell you!'

12 George in trouble

'What's the matter?' asked George, as the three children tore up to her. 'Has something happened?'

'Yes, George. Someone has taken three most important pages out of your father's book!' panted Julian. 'And broken the test-tubes he was making an experiment with. Mr Roland thinks you might have had something to do with it!'

'The beast!' said George, her blue eyes deepening with anger. 'As if I'd do a thing like that! Why should he think it's me, anyway?'

'Well, George, you left that bottle of oil in the study fender,' said Anne. 'I haven't told anyone at all what you told me happened last night – but somehow Mr Roland guessed you had something to do with the bottle of oil.'

'Didn't you tell the boys how I got Timmy indoors?' asked George. 'Well, there's nothing much to tell, Julian. I just heard poor old Tim coughing in the night, and I half-dressed, went down, and took him into the study, where there was a fire. Mother keeps a bottle of oil that she used to rub her chest with when she has a cough – so I thought it might do Timmy's cold good, too. I got the oil and rubbed him well – and we both fell asleep by the fire till six o'clock. I was sleepy when I woke up, and forgot the oil. That's all.'

'And you didn't take any pages from the book Uncle

Quentin is writing, and you didn't break anything in the study, did you?' said Anne.

'Of course not, silly,' said George, indignantly. 'How can you ask me a thing like that? You must be mad.'

George never told a lie, and the others always believed her, whatever she said. They stared at her, and she stared back.

'I wonder who could have taken those pages then?' said Julian. 'Maybe your father will come across them, after all. I expect he put them into some safe place and then forgot all about them. And the test-tubes might easily have over-balanced and broken themselves. Some of them look very shaky to me.'

'I suppose I shall get into trouble now for taking Tim into the study,' said George.

'And for not coming into lessons this morning,' said Dick. 'You really are an idiot, George. I never knew anyone like you for walking right into trouble.'

'Hadn't you better stay out a bit longer, till everyone has calmed down a bit?' said Anne.

'No,' said George at once. 'If I'm going to get into a row, I'll get into it now! *I'm* not afraid!'

She marched over the cliff path, with Timmy running round her as usual. The others followed. It wasn't nice to think that George was going to get into such trouble.

They came to the house and went up the path. Mr Roland saw them from the window and opened the door. He glanced at George.

'Your father wants to see you in the study,' said the tutor. Then he turned to the others, looking annoyed.

'Why did you go out without me? I meant to go with you.'

'Oh did you, sir? I'm sorry,' said Julian, politely, not

looking at Mr Roland. 'We just went out on the cliff a little way.'

'Georgina, did you go into the study last night?' asked Mr Roland, watching George as she took off her hat and coat.

'I'll answer my father's questions, not yours,' said George.

'What you want is a good telling off,' said Mr Roland. 'And if I were your father I'd give it to you!'

'You're not my father,' answered George. She went to the study door and opened it. There was no one there.

'Father isn't here,' said George.

'He'll be there in a minute,' said Mr Roland. 'Go in and wait. And you others, go up and wash for lunch.'

The other three children felt almost as if they were deserting George as they went up the stairs. They could hear Timmy whining from the yard outside. He knew his little mistress was in trouble, and he wanted to be with her.

George sat down on a chair, and gazed at the fire, remembering how she had sat on the rug there with Tim last night, rubbing his hairy chest. How silly of her to have forgotten the bottle of oil!

Her father came into the room, frowning and angry. He looked sternly at George.

'Were you in here last night, George?' he asked.

'Yes, I was,' answered George at once.

'What were you doing in here?' asked her father. 'You know you children are forbidden to come into my study.'

'I know,' said George. 'But you see Timmy had a dreadful cough, and I couldn't bear it. So I crept down about one o'clock and let him in. This was the only room that was really warm, so I sat here and rubbed his chest with the oil Mother uses when she has a cold.'

'Rubbed the dog's chest with camphorated oil!' exclaimed her father, in amazement. 'What a mad thing to do! As if it would do him any good.'

'It didn't seem mad to me,' said George. 'It seemed sensible. And Timmy's cough is much better today. I'm sorry for coming into the study. I didn't touch a thing, of course.'

'George, something very serious has happened,' said her father, looking gravely at her. 'Some of my test-tubes with which I was doing an important experiment, have been broken – and, worse than that, three pages of my book have gone. Tell me on your honour that you know nothing of these things.'

'I know nothing of them,' said George, looking her father straight in the eyes. Her own eyes shone very blue and clear as she gazed at him. He felt quite certain that George was speaking the truth. She could know nothing of the damage done. Then where were those pages?

'George, last night when I went to bed at eleven o'clock, everything was in order,' he said. 'I read over those three important pages and checked them once more myself. This morning they are gone.'

'Then they must have been taken between eleven o'clock and one o'clock,' said George. 'I was here from that time until six.'

'But *who* could have taken them?' said her father. 'The window was fastened, as far as I know. And nobody knows that those three pages were so important but myself. It is most extraordinary.'

'Mr Roland probably knew,' said George, slowly.

'Don't be absurd,' said her father. 'Even if he did realise they were important, he would not have taken them. He's a very decent fellow. And that reminds me – why were you not at lessons this morning, George?'

'I'm not going to do lessons any more with Mr Roland,' said George. 'I simply hate him!'

'George! I will *not* have you talking like this!' said her father. 'Do you want me to say you are to lose Tim altogether?'

'No,' said George, feeling shaky about the knees. 'And I don't think it's fair to keep trying to force me to do things by threatening me with losing Timothy. If – if – you do a thing like that – I'll – I'll run away or something!'

There were no tears in George's eyes. She sat bolt upright on her chair, gazing defiantly at her father. How difficult she was! Her father sighed, and remembered that he too in his own childhood had been called 'difficult'. Perhaps George took after him. She could be so good and sweet – and here she was being perfectly impossible!

Her father did not know what to do with George. He thought he had better have a word with his wife. He got up and went to the door.

'Stay here. I shall be back in a moment. I want to speak to your mother about you.'

'Don't speak to Mr Roland about me, will you?' said George, who felt quite certain that the tutor would urge terrible punishments for her and Timmy. 'Oh, Father, if only Timothy had been in the house last night, sleeping in my room as usual, he would have heard whoever it was that stole your secret – and he would have barked and roused the house!'

Her father said nothing, but he knew that what George had said was true. Timmy wouldn't have let anyone get into the study. It was funny he hadn't barked in the night, if anyone from outside had climbed in at the study window. Still, it was the other side of the house. Maybe he had heard nothing.

The door closed. George sat still on her chair, gazing up at the mantelpiece, where a clock ticked away the time. She felt very miserable. Everything was going wrong, every single thing!

As she gazed at the panelled overmantel, she counted the wooden panels. There were eight. Now, where had she heard of eight panels before? Of course – in that Secret Way. There were eight panels marked on the roll of linen. What a pity there had not been eight panels in a wooden overmantel at Kirrin Farmhouse!

George glanced out of the window, and wondered if it faced east. She looked to see where the sun was – it was not shining into the room – but it did in the early morning – so it must face east. Fancy – here was a room facing east and with eight wooden panels. She wondered if it had a stone floor.

The floor was covered with a large thick carpet. George got up and went to the wall. She pulled up the edge of the carpet there – and saw that the floor underneath was made of large flat stones. The study had a stone floor too!

She sat down again and gazed at the wooden panels, trying to remember which one in the roll of linen was marked with a cross. But of course it couldn't be a room in Kirrin Cottage – it must be in Kirrin Farmhouse where the Secret Way began.

But just suppose it *was* Kirrin Cottage! Certainly the directions had been found in Kirrin Farmhouse – but that was not to say that the Secret Way had to begin there, even though Mrs Sanders seemed to think it did.

George was feeling excited. 'I must tap round about

those eight panels and try to find the one that is marked on the linen roll,' she thought. 'It may slide back or something, and I shall suddenly see the entrance opening!'

She got up to try her luck – but at that moment the door opened again and her father came in looking very grave.

'I have been talking to your mother,' he said. 'She agrees with me that you have been very disobedient, rude and defiant. We can't let behaviour like that pass, George. You will have to be punished.'

George looked anxiously at her father. If only her punishment had nothing to do with Timothy! But, of course, it had.

'You will go to bed for the rest of the day, and you will not see Timothy for three days,' said her father. 'I will get Julian to feed him and take him for a walk. If you persist in being defiant, Timothy will have to go away altogether. I am afraid, strange as it may seem, that that dog has a bad influence on you.'

'He hasn't, he hasn't!' cried George. 'Oh, he'll be so miserable if I don't see him for three whole days.'

'There's nothing more to be said,' said her father. 'Go straight upstairs to bed, and think over all I have said to you, George. I am very disappointed in your behaviour these holidays. I really did think the influence of your three cousins had made you into a normal, sensible girl. Now you are worse then you have ever been.'

He held open the door and George walked out, holding her head high. She heard the others having their dinner in the dining-room. She went straight upstairs and undressed. She got into bed and thought miserably of not seeing Tim for three days. She couldn't bear it! Nobody could possibly know how much she loved Timothy!

Joanna came up with a tray of dinner. 'Well, it's a pity to see you in bed,' she said cheerfully. 'Now you be a sensible girl and behave properly and you'll soon be downstairs again.'

George picked at her dinner. She did not feel at all hungry. She lay back on the bed, thinking of Tim and thinking of the eight panels over the mantelpiece. Could they possibly be the ones shown in the Secret Way directions? She gazed out of the window and thought hard.

'Golly, it's snowing!' she said suddenly, sitting up. 'I thought it would when I saw that leaden sky this morning. It's snowing hard! It will be quite thick by tonight – inches deep. Oh, poor Timothy. I hope Julian will see that his kennel is kept clear of the drifting snow.'

George had plenty of time to think as she lay in bed. Joanna came and took the tray away. No one else came to see her. George felt sure the other children had been forbidden to go up and speak to her. She felt lonely and left-out.

She thought of her father's lost pages. Could Mr Roland have taken them? After all, he was very interested in her father's work and seemed to understand it. The thief must have been someone who knew which were the important pages. Surely Timothy would have barked if a thief had come in from outside, even though the study was the other side of the house. Timmy had such sharp ears.

'I think it must have been someone *in*side the house,' said George. 'None of us children, that's certain – and not Mother or Joanna. So that only leaves Mr Roland. And I did find him in the study that other night when Timmy woke me by growling.'

She sat up in bed suddenly. 'I believe Mr Roland had Timothy put out of the house because he wanted to go poking round the study again and was afraid Tim would bark!' she thought. 'He was so very insistent that Tim should go out of doors – even when everyone else begged for me to have him indoors. I believe – I really do believe – that Mr Roland is the thief!'

The little girl felt very excited. Could it be that the tutor had stolen the pages – and broken those important test-tubes? How she wished that the others would come and see her, so that she could talk things over with them!

13 Julian has a surprise

The three children downstairs felt very sorry for George. Uncle Quentin had forbidden them to go up and see her.

'A little time for thinking out things all alone may do George good,' he said.

'Poor old George,' said Julian. 'It's too bad, isn't it? I say – look at the snow!'

The snow was falling very thickly. Julian went to the window and looked out. 'I shall have to go and see that Timmy's kennel is all right,' he said. 'We don't want the poor old fellow to be snowed up! I expect he is wondering what the snow is!'

Timothy was certainly very puzzled to see everywhere covered with soft white stuff. He sat in his kennel and stared out at the falling flakes, his big brown eyes following them as they fell to the ground. He was puzzled and unhappy. Why was he living out here by himself in the cold? Why didn't George come to him? Didn't she love him any more? The big dog was very miserable, as miserable as George!

He was delighted to see Julian. He jumped up at the boy and licked his face. 'Good old Tim!' said Julian. 'Are you all right? Let me sweep away some of this snow and swing your kennel round a bit so that no flakes fly inside. There – that's better. No, we're not going for a walk, old thing – not now.'

The boy patted the dog and fussed him a bit, then

went indoors. The others met him at the sitting-room door.

'Julian! Mr Roland is going out for a walk by himself. Aunt Fanny is lying down, and Uncle Quentin is in his study. Can't we go up and see George?'

'We were forbidden to,' said Julian, doubtfully.

'I know,' said Dick. 'But I don't mind risking it for the sake of making George feel a bit happier. It must be so awful for her, lying up there all alone, knowing she can't see Tim for days.'

'Well – let me go up, as I'm the eldest,' said Julian. 'You two stay down here in the sitting-room and talk. Then Uncle Quentin will think we're all here. I'll slip up and see George for a few minutes.'

'All right,' said Dick. 'Give her our love and tell her we'll look after Timmy.'

Julian slipped quietly up the stairs. He opened George's door and crept inside. He shut the door, and saw George sitting up in bed, looking at him in delight.

'Sh!' said Julian. 'I'm not supposed to be here!'

'Oh Julian!' said George joyfully. 'How good of you to come. I was so lonely. Come this side of the bed. Then if anyone comes in suddenly, you can duck down and hide.'

Julian went to the other side of the bed. George began to pour out to him all she had been thinking of.

'I believe Mr Roland is the thief, I really do!' she said. 'I'm not saying that because I hate him, Julian, really I'm not. After all, I *did* find him snooping round the study one afternoon – and again in the middle of the night. He may have got to hear of my father's work, and come to see if he could steal it. It was just lucky for him that we needed a tutor. I'm sure he stole those pages, and I'm sure he wanted Timmy out of the house so that he could do his stealing without Tim hearing him and growling.'

'Oh, George – I don't think so,' said Julian, who really could not approve of the idea of the tutor doing such a thing. 'It all sounds so far-fetched and un-believable.'

'Lots of unbelievable things happen,' said George. 'Lots. And this is one of them.'

'Well, if Mr Roland *did* steal the pages, they must be somewhere in the house,' said Julian. 'He hasn't been out all day. They must be somewhere in his bedroom.'

'Of course!' said George, looking thrilled. 'I wish he'd go out! Then I'd search his room.'

'George, you can't do things like that,' said Julian, quite shocked.

'You simply don't know what things I can do, if I really want to,' said George, setting her mouth in a firm line. 'Oh – what's that noise?'

There was the bang of a door. Julian went cautiously to the window and peeped out. The snow had stopped falling for a time, and Mr Roland had taken the chance of going out.

'It's Mr Roland,' said Julian.

'Oooh – I could search his room now, if you'll keep watch at the window and tell me if he comes back,' said George, throwing back the bedclothes at once.

'No, George, don't,' said Julian. 'Honestly and truly, it's awful to search somebody's room like that. And anyway, I dare say he's got the pages with him. He may even be going to give them to somebody!'

'I never thought of that,' said George, and she looked at Julian with wide eyes. 'Isn't that sickening? Of course he may be doing that. He knows those two artists at Kirrin Farmhouse, for instance. They may be in the plot too.'

'Oh, George, don't be silly,' said Julian. 'You are making a mountain out of a mole-hill, talking of plots and goodness knows what! Anyone would think we were in the middle of a big adventure.'

'Well, I think we are,' said George, unexpectedly, and she looked rather solemn. 'I sort of feel it all round me – a Big Adventure!'

Julian stared at his cousin thoughtfully. Could there possibly be anything in what she said?

'Julian, will you do something for me?' said George.

'Of course,' said the boy, at once.

'Go out and follow Mr Roland,' said George. 'Don't let him see you. There's a white macintosh in the hall cupboard. Put it on and you won't be easily seen against the snow. Follow him and see if he meets anyone and gives them anything that looks like the pages of my father's book – you know those big pages he writes on. They're very large.'

'All right,' said Julian. 'But if I do, promise you won't go and search his room. You can't do things like that, George.'

'I can,' said George. 'But I won't, if you'll just follow Mr Roland for me. I'm sure he's going to hand over what he has stolen to others who are in the plot! And I bet those others will be the two artists at Kirrin Farmhouse that he pretended not to know!'

'You'll find you're quite wrong,' said Julian, going to the door. 'I'm sure I shan't be able to follow Mr Roland, anyway – he's been gone five minutes now!'

'Yes, you will, silly – he'll have left his footmarks in the snow,' said George. 'And oh, Julian – I quite forgot to tell you something else exciting. Oh dear, there isn't time now. I'll tell you when you come back, if you can come up again then. It's about the Secret Way.'

'Really?' said Julian, in delight. It had been a great disappointment to him that all their hunting and searching had come to nothing. 'All right – I'll try and creep up again later. If I don't come, you'll know I can't, and you must wait till bed-time.'

He disappeared and shut the door quietly. He slipped downstairs, popped his head into the sitting-room and whispered to the others that he was going out after the tutor.

'Tell you why, later,' he said. He put the white macintosh around him and went out into the garden. Snow was beginning to fall again, but not yet heavily enough to hide Mr Roland's deep footsteps. He had had big wellington boots on, and the footmarks showed up well in the six-inch-deep snow.

The boy followed them quickly. The countryside was very wintry-looking now. The sky was low and leaden, and he could see there was much more snow to come. He hurried on after Mr Roland, though he could not see a sign of the tutor.

Down the lane and over the path that led across the common went the double row of footmarks. Julian stumbled on, his eyes glued to the foot-prints. Suddenly he heard the sound of voices and stopped. A big gorse bush lay to the right and the voices came from there. The boy went nearer to the bush. He heard his tutor's voice, talking in low tones. He could not hear a word that was said.

'Whoever can he be talking to?' he wondered. He crept up closer to the bush. There was a hollow space inside. Julian thought he could creep right into it, though it would be very prickly, and peer out of the other side. Carefully the boy crept into the prickly hollow, where the branches were bare and brown.

He parted the prickly branches slowly and cautiously – and to his amazement he saw Mr Roland talking to the two artists from Kirrin Farmhouse – Mr Thomas and Mr Wilton! So George was right. The tutor had met them – and, as Julian watched, Mr Roland handed over to Mr Thomas a doubled-up sheaf of papers.

'They look just like pages from Uncle Quentin's book,' said Julian to himself. 'I say – this is mighty strange. It does begin to look like a plot – with Mr Roland at the centre of it!'

Mr Thomas put the papers into the pocket of his overcoat. The men muttered a few more words, which even Julian's sharp ears could not catch, and then parted. The artists went off towards Kirrin Farmhouse, and Mr Roland took the path back over the common. Julian crouched down in the hollow of the prickly gorse bush, hoping the tutor would not turn and see him. Luckily he didn't. He went straight on and disappeared into the snow, which was now falling thickly. It was also beginning to get dark and Julian, unable to see the path very clearly, hurried after Mr Roland, half-afraid of being lost in the snow-storm.

Mr Roland was not anxious to be out longer than he could help, either. He almost ran back to Kirrin Cottage. He came to the gate at last, and Julian watched him go into the house. He gave him a little time to take off his things and then, giving Timothy a pat as he went by, he went to the garden door. He took off his macintosh, changed his boots, and slipped into the sitting-room before Mr Roland had come down from his bedroom.

'What's happened?' asked Dick and Anne, seeing that Julian was in a great state of excitement. But he could not tell them, for just then Joanna came in to lay the tea.

Much to Julian's disappointment, he could not say a word to the others all that evening, because one or other of the grown-ups was always in the room. Neither could he go up to see George. He could hardly wait to tell his news, but it was no good, he had to.

'Is it still snowing, Aunt Fanny?' asked Anne.

Her aunt went to the front door and looked out. The snow was piled high against the step!

'Yes,' she said, when she came back. 'It is snowing fast and thickly. If it goes on like this we shall be completely snowed up, as we were two winters ago! We couldn't get out of the house for five days then. The milkman couldn't get to us, nor the baker. Fortunately we had plenty of tinned milk, and I can bake my own bread. You poor children, you will not be able to go out tomorrow – the snow will be too thick!'

'Will Kirrin Farmhouse be snowed up too?' asked Mr Roland.

'Oh yes – worse than we shall be,' said Aunt Fanny. 'But they won't mind! They have plenty of food there. They will be prisoners just as much, and more, as we shall.'

Julian wondered why Mr Roland had asked that question. Was he afraid that his friends would not be able to send those pages away by the post – or take them anywhere by bus or car? The boy felt certain this was the reason for the question. How he longed to be able to talk over everything with the others.

'I'm tired!' he said, about eight o'clock. 'Let's go to bed.'

Dick and Anne stared at him in astonishment. Usually, as he was the eldest, he went to bed last of all. Tonight he was actually *asking* to go! Julian winked quickly at them, and they backed him up at once.

Dick yawned widely, and so did Anne. Their aunt put down the sewing she was doing. 'You *do* sound tired!' she said. 'I think you'd better all go to bed.'

'Could I just go out and see if Timmy is all right?' asked Julian. His aunt nodded. The boy put on his rubber boots and coat, and slipped out through the garden door into the yard. It was very deep in snow, too. Tim's kennel was half-hidden in it. The dog had trampled a space in front of the kennel door, and stood there, looking for Julian as he came out of the house.

'Poor old boy, out here in the snow all alone,' said Julian. He patted the dog, and Timmy whined. He was asking to go back with the boy.

'I wish I *could* take you back with me,' said Julian. 'Never mind, Timothy. I'll come and see you tomorrow.'

He went indoors again. The children said good-night to their aunt and Mr Roland, and went upstairs.

'Undress quickly, put on dressing-gowns and meet in George's room,' whispered Julian to the others. 'Don't make a sound or we'll have Aunt Fanny up. Quick now!'

In less than three minutes the children were undressed, and were sitting on George's bed. She was very pleased to see them. Anne slipped into bed with her, because her feet were cold.

'Julian! Did you follow Mr Roland all right?' whispered George.

'Why did he follow him?' asked Dick, who had been dying to know.

Julian told them everything as quickly as he could – all that George suspected – and how he had followed the tutor – and what he had seen. When George heard how Julian had watched him giving a sheaf of papers to the two artists, her eyes gleamed angrily.

'The thief! They must have been the lost pages! And to think my father has been so friendly to him. Oh, what can we do? Those men will get the papers away as quickly as they can, and the secret Father has been working on for ages will be used by someone else – for some other country, probably!'

'They can't get the papers away,' said Julian. 'You've no idea how thick the snow is now, George. We shall be prisoners here for a few days, if this snow goes on, and so will the people in Kirrin Farmhouse. If they want to hide the papers, they will have to hide them in the farmhouse! If only we could get over there and hunt round!'

'Well, we can't,' said Dick. 'That's quite certain. We'd be up to our necks in snow!'

The four children looked gloomily at one another. Dick and Anne could hardly believe that the jolly Mr Roland was a thief – a spy perhaps, trying to steal a valuable secret from a friendly scientist. And they couldn't stop it.

'We'd better tell your father,' said Julian at last.

'No,' said Anne. 'He wouldn't believe it, would he, George?'

'He'd laugh at us and go straight and tell Mr Roland,' said George. 'That would warn him, and he mustn't be warned. He mustn't know that we guess anything.'

'Sh! Aunt Fanny's coming!' whispered Dick, suddenly. The boys slipped out of the room and into bed. Anne hopped across to her own little bed. All was peace and quiet when the children's aunt came into the bedroom.

She said good-night and tucked them up. As soon as

she had gone down, the four children met together again in George's room.

'George, tell me now what you were going to say about the Secret Way,' said Julian.

'Oh, yes,' said George. 'Well, there may be nothing in my idea at all – but in the study downstairs, there are eight wooden panels over the mantelpiece – and the floor is of stone – and the room faces east! A bit odd, isn't it? Just what the directions said.'

'Is there a cupboard there too?' asked Julian.

'No. But there is everything else,' said George. 'And I was just wondering if by any chance the entrance to the Secret Way is in this house, not in the farmhouse. After all, they both belonged to my family at one time, you know. The people living in the farmhouse years ago must have known all about this cottage.'

'Golly, George – suppose the entrance *was* here!' said Dick. 'Wouldn't it be simply marvellous! Let's go straight down and look!'

'Don't be silly,' said Julian. 'Go down to the study when Uncle Quentin is there? I'd rather meet twenty lions than face Uncle! Especially after what has happened!'

'Well, we simply MUST find out if George's idea is right; we simply must,' said Dick, forgetting to whisper.

'Shut up, idiot!' said Julian, giving him a punch. 'Do you want to bring the whole household up here?'

'Sorry!' said Dick. 'But, oh golly, this *is* exciting. It's an Adventure again.'

'Just what I said,' said George, eagerly. 'Listen, shall we wait till midnight, and then creep down to the study when everyone is asleep, and try our luck? There may be nothing in my idea at all – but we'll have to find out now. I don't believe I could go to sleep till I've tried each one of those panels over the mantelpiece to see if something happens.'

'Well, I know I can't sleep a wink either,' said Dick. 'Listen – is that someone coming up? We'd better go. Come on, Julian! We'll meet in George's room at midnight – and creep down and try out George's idea!'

The two boys went off to their own room. Neither of them could sleep a wink. Nor could George. She lay awake, and went over and over in her mind all that had happened those holidays. 'It's like a jigsaw puzzle,' she thought. 'I couldn't understand a lot of things at first – but now they are fitting together, and making a picture.'

Anne was fast asleep. She had to be awakened at midnight. 'Come on!' whispered Julian, shaking her. 'Don't you want to share in this adventure?'

14   The Secret Way at last!

The four children crept downstairs through the dark and silent night. Nobody made a sound at all. They made their way to the study. George softly closed the door and then switched on the light.

The children stared at the eight panels over the mantelpiece. Yes – there were exactly eight, four in one row and four in the row above. Julian spread the linen roll out on the table, and the children pored over it.

'The cross is in the middle of the second panel in the top row,' said Julian in a low voice. 'I'll try pressing it. Watch, all of you!'

He went to the fireplace. The others followed him, their hearts beating fast with excitement. Julian stood on tiptoe and began to press hard in the middle of the second panel. Nothing happened.

'Press harder! Tap it!' said Dick.

'I daren't make too much noise,' said Julian, feeling all over the panel to see if there was any roughness that might tell of a hidden spring or lever.

Suddenly, under his hands, the panel slid silently back, just as the one had done at Kirrin Farmhouse in the hall! The children stared at the space behind, thrilled.

'It's not big enough to get into,' said George. 'It can't be the entrance to the Secret Way.'

Julian got out his torch from his dressing-gown

pocket. He put it inside the opening, and gave a low exclamation.

'There's a sort of handle here – with strong wire or something attached to it. I'll pull it and see what happens.'

He pulled – but he was not strong enough to move the handle that seemed to be embedded in the wall. Dick put his hand in and the two boys then pulled together.

'It's moving – it's giving way a bit,' panted Julian. 'Go on, Dick, pull hard!'

The handle suddenly came away from the wall, and behind it came thick wire, rusty and old. At the same time a curious grating noise came from below the hearthrug in front of the fireplace, and Anne almost fell.

'Julian! Something is moving under the rug!' she said, frightened. 'I felt it. Under the rug, quick!'

The handle could not be pulled out any farther. The boys let go, and looked down. To the right of the fireplace, under the rug, something had moved. There was no doubt of that. The rug sagged down instead of being flat and straight.

'A stone has moved in the floor,' said Julian, his voice shaking with excitement. 'This handle works a lever, which is attached to this wire. Quick – pull up the rug, and roll back the carpet.'

With trembling hands the children pulled back the rug and the carpet – and then stood staring at a very strange thing. A big flat stone laid in the floor had slipped downwards, pulled in some manner by the wire attached to the handle hidden behind the panel! There was now a black space where the stone had been.

'Look at that!' said George, in a thrilling whisper.

'The entrance to the Secret Way!'

'It's here after all!' said Julian.

'Let's go down!' said Dick.

'No!' said Anne, shivering at the thought of disappearing into the black hole.

Julian flashed his torch into the black space. The stone had slid down and then sideways. Below was a space just big enough to take a man, bending down.

'I expect there's a passage or something leading from here, under the house, and out,' said Julian. 'Golly, I wonder where it leads to?'

'We simply must find out,' said George.

'Not now,' said Dick. 'It's dark and cold. I don't fancy going along the Secret Way at midnight. I don't mind just hopping down to see what it's like – but don't let's go along any passage till tomorrow.'

'Uncle Quentin will be working here tomorrow,' said Julian.

'He said he was going to sweep the snow away from the front door in the morning,' said George. 'We could slip into the study then. It's Saturday. There may be no lessons.'

'All right,' said Julian, who badly wanted to explore everything then and there. 'But for goodness' sake let's have a look and see if there *is* a passage down there. At present all we can see is a hole!'

'I'll help you down,' said Dick. So he gave his brother a hand and the boy dropped lightly down into the black space, holding his torch. He gave a loud exclamation.

'It's the entrance to the Secret Way all right! There's a passage leading from here under the house – awfully low and narrow – but I can see it's a passage. I do wonder where it leads to!'

He shivered. It was cold and damp down there.

'Give me a hand up, Dick,' he said. He was soon out of the hole and in the warm study again.

The children looked at one another in the greatest joy and excitement. This *was* an Adventure, a real Adventure. It was a pity they couldn't go on with it now.

'We'll try and take Timmy with us tomorrow,' said George. 'Oh, I say – how are we going to shut the entrance up?'

'We can't leave the rug and carpet sagging over that hole,' said Dick. 'Nor can we leave the panel open.'

'We'll see if we can get the stone back,' said Julian. He stood on tiptoe and felt about inside the panel. His hand closed on a kind of knob, set deep in a stone. He pulled it, and at once the handle slid back, pulled by the wire. At the same time the sunk stone glided to the surface of the floor again, making a slight grating sound as it did so.

'Well, it's like magic!' said Dick. 'It really is! Fancy the mechanism working so smoothly after years of not being used. This is the most exciting thing I've ever seen!'

There was a noise in the bedroom above. The children stood still and listened.

'It's Mr Roland!' whispered Dick. 'He's heard us. Quick, slip upstairs before he comes down.'

They switched out the light and opened the study door softly. Up the stairs they fled, as quietly as church mice, their hearts thumping so loudly that it seemed as if everyone in the house must hear the beat.

The girls got safely to their rooms and Dick was able to slip into his. But Julian was seen by Mr Roland as he came out of his room with a torch.

'What are you doing, Julian!' asked the tutor, in

surprise. 'Did you hear a noise downstairs? I thought I did.'

'Yes – I heard quite a lot of noise downstairs,' said Julian, truthfully. 'But perhaps it's snow falling off the roof, landing with a plop in the ground, sir. Do you think that's it?'

'I don't know,' said the tutor doubtfully. 'We'll go down and see.'

They went down, but of course there was nothing to be seen. Julian was glad they had been able to shut the panel and make the stone come back to its proper place again. Mr Roland was the very last person he wanted to tell his secret to.

They went upstairs and Julian slipped into his room. 'Is it all right?' whispered Dick.

'Yes,' said Julian. 'Don't let's talk. Mr Roland's awake, and I don't want him to suspect anything.'

The boys fell asleep. When they awoke in the morning, there was a completely white world outside. Snow covered everything and covered it deeply. Timothy's kennel could not be seen! But there were footmarks round about it.

George gave a squeal when she saw how deep the snow was. 'Poor Timothy! I'm going to get him in. I don't care what anyone says! I won't let him be buried in the snow!'

She dressed and tore downstairs. She went out to the kennel, floundering knee deep in the snow. But there was no Timmy there!

A loud bark from the kitchen made her jump. Joanna the cook knocked on the kitchen window. 'It's all right! I couldn't bear the dog out there in the snow, so I fetched him in, poor thing. Your mother says I can have him in the kitchen but you're not to come and see him.'

'Oh, good – Timmy's in the warmth!' said George, gladly. She yelled to Joanna, 'Thanks awfully! You *are* kind!'

She went indoors and told the others. They were very glad. 'And *I've* got a bit of news for *you*,' said Dick. 'Mr Roland is in bed with a bad cold, so there are to be no lessons today. Cheers!'

'Golly, that *is* good news,' said George, cheering up tremendously. 'Timmy in the warm kitchen and Mr Roland kept in bed. I do feel pleased!'

'We shall be able to explore the Secret Way safely now,' said Julian. 'Aunt Fanny is going to do something in the kitchen this morning with Joanna, and Uncle is going to tackle the snow. I vote we say we'll do lessons by ourselves in the sitting-room, and then, when everything is safe, we'll explore the Secret Way!'

'But why must we do lessons?' asked George in dismay.

'Because if we don't, silly, we'll have to help your father dig away the snow,' said Julian.

So, to his uncle's surprise, Julian suggested that the four children should do lessons by themselves in the sitting-room. 'Well, I thought you'd like to come and help dig away the snow,' said Uncle Quentin. 'But perhaps you had better get on with your work.'

The children sat themselves down as good as gold in the sitting-room, their books before them. They heard Mr Roland coughing in his room. They heard their aunt go into the kitchen and talk to Joanna. They heard Timmy scratching at the kitchen door – then paws pattering down the passage – then a big, inquiring nose came round the door, and there was old Timmy, looking anxiously for his beloved mistress!

'Timmy!' squealed George, and ran to him. She flung her arms round his neck and hugged him.

'You act as if you hadn't seen Tim for a year,' said Julian.

'It seems like a year,' said George. 'I say, there's my father digging away like mad. Can't we go to the study now? We ought to be safe for a good while.'

They left the sitting-room and went to the study. Julian was soon pulling the handle behind the secret panel. George had already turned back the rug and the carpet. The stone slid downward and sideways. The Secret Way was open!

'Come on!' said Julian. 'Hurry!'

He jumped down into the hole. Dick followed, then Anne, then George. Julian pushed them all into the narrow, low passage. Then he looked up. Perhaps he had better pull the carpet and rug over the hole, in case anyone came into the room and looked around. It took him a few seconds to do it. Then he bent down and joined the others in the passage. They were going to explore the Secret Way at last!

15 An exciting journey and hunt

Timothy had leapt down into the hole when George had jumped. He now ran ahead of the children, puzzled at their wanting to explore such a cold, dark place. Both Julian and Dick had torches, which threw broad beams before them.

There was not much to be seen. The Secret Way under the old house was narrow and low, so that the children were forced to go in single file, and to stoop almost double. It was a great relief to them when the passage became a little wider, and the room a little higher. It was very tiring to stoop all the time.

'Have you any idea where the Secret Way is going?' Dick asked Julian. 'I mean – is it going towards the sea, or away from it?'

'Oh, not towards the sea!' said Julian, who had a very good sense of direction. 'As far as I can make out the passage is going towards the common. Look at the walls – they are rather sandy in places, and we know the common has sandy soil. I hope we shan't find that the passage has fallen in anywhere.'

They went on and on. The Secret Way was very straight, though occasionally it would round a rocky part in a curve.

'Isn't it dark and cold?' said Anne, shivering. 'I wish I had put on a coat. How many miles have we come, Julian?'

'Not even one, silly!' said Julian. 'Hallo – look here – the passage has fallen in a bit there!'

Two bright torches shone in front of them and the children saw that the sandy roof had fallen in. Julian kicked at the pile of sandy soil with his foot.

'It's all right,' he said. 'We can force our way through easily. It isn't much of a fall, and it's mostly sand. I'll do a bit of kicking!'

After some trampling and kicking, the roof-fall no longer blocked the way. There was now enough room for the children to climb over it, bending their heads low to avoid knocking them against the top of the passage. Julian shone his torch forward, and saw that the way was clear.

'The Secret Way is very wide just here!' he said suddenly, and flashed his torch around to show the others.

'It's been widened out to make a sort of little room,' said George. 'Look, there's a kind of bench at the back, made out of the rock. I believe it's a resting-place.'

George was right. It was very tiring to creep along the narrow passage for so long. The little wide place with its rocky bench made a very good resting-place. The four tired children, cold but excited, huddled together on the funny seat and took a welcome rest. Timmy put his head on George's knee. He was delighted to be with her again.

'Well, come on,' said Julian, after a few minutes. 'I'm getting awfully cold. I do wonder where this passage comes out!'

'Julian – do you think it could come out at Kirrin Farmhouse?' asked George, suddenly. 'You know what Mrs Sanders said – that there was a secret passage leading from the farmhouse somewhere. Well, this may be the one – and it leads to Kirrin Cottage!'

'George, I believe you're right!' said Julian. 'Yes – the two houses belonged to your family years ago! And in the old days there were often secret passages joining houses, so it's quite plain this secret way joins them up together! Why didn't I think of that before?'

'I say!' squealed Anne, in a high, excited voice, 'I say! I've thought of something too!'

'What?' asked everyone.

'Well – if those two artists have got Uncle's papers, we may be able to get them away before the men can send them off by post, or take them away themselves!' squeaked Anne, so thrilled with her idea that she could hardly get the words out quickly enough. 'They're prisoners at the farmhouse because of the snow, just as we were at the cottage.'

'*Anne!* You're right!' said Julian.

'Clever girl!' said Dick.

'I *say* – if we *could* get those papers again – how wonderful it would be!' said George. Timmy joined in the general excitement, and jumped up and down in joy. Something had pleased the children, so he was pleased too!

'Come on!' said Julian, taking Anne's hand. 'This is thrilling. If George is right, and this Secret Way comes out at Kirrin Farmhouse somewhere, we'll somehow hunt through those men's rooms and find the papers.'

'You said that searching people's rooms was a shocking thing to do,' said George.

'Well, I didn't know then all I know now,' said Julian. 'We're doing this for your father – and maybe for our country too, if his secret formula is valuable. We've got to set our wits to work now, to outwit dangerous enemies.'

'Do you really think they are dangerous?' asked Anne rather afraid.

'Yes, I should think so,' said Julian. 'But you needn't worry, Anne, you've got me and Dick and Tim to protect you.'

'I can protect her too,' said George, indignantly.

'You're fiercer than any boy I know!' said Dick.

'Come on,' said Julian, impatiently. 'I'm longing to get to the end of this passage.'

They all went on again, Anne following behind Julian, and Dick behind George. Timmy ran up and down the line, squeezing by them whenever he wanted to. He thought it was a very peculiar way to spend a morning!

Julian stopped suddenly, after they had gone a good way. 'What's up?' asked Dick, from the back. 'Not another roof-fall, I hope!'

'No – but I think we've come to the end of the passage!' said Julian, thrilled. The others crowded as close to him as they could. The passage certainly had come to an end. There was a rocky wall in front of them, and set firmly in it were iron staples intended for footholds. These went up the wall and when Julian turned his torch upwards, the children saw that there was a square opening in the roof of the passage.

'We have to climb up this rocky wall now,' said Julian, 'go through that dark hole there, keep on climbing – and goodness knows where we come out! I'll go first. You wait here, everyone, and I'll come back and tell you what I've seen.'

The boy put his torch between his teeth, and then pulled himself up by the iron staples set in the wall. He set his feet on them, and then climbed up through the square dark hole, feeling for the staples as he went.

He went up for a good way. It was almost like going up a chimney shaft, he thought. It was cold and smelt musty.

Suddenly he came to a ledge, and he stepped on to it. He took his torch from his teeth and flashed it around him.

There was a stone wall behind him, at the side of him and stone above him. The black hole up which he had come, yawned by his feet. Julian shone his torch in front of him, and a shock of surprise went through him.

There was no stone wall in front of him, but a big wooden door, made of black oak. A handle was set about waist-high; Julian turned it with trembling fingers. What was he going to see?

The door opened outwards, over the ledge, and it was difficult to get round it without falling back into the hole. Julian managed to open it wide, squeezed round it without losing his footing, and stepped beyond it, expecting to find himself in a room.

But his hand felt more wood in front of him! He shone his torch round, and found that he was up against what looked like yet another door. Under his searching fingers it suddenly moved sideways, and slid silently away!

And then Julian knew where he was! 'I'm in the cupboard at Kirrin Farmhouse – the one that has a false back!' he thought. 'The Secret Way comes up behind it! How clever! Little did we know when we played about in this cupboard that not only did it have a sliding back, but that it was the entrance to the Secret Way, hidden behind it!'

The cupboard was now full of clothes belonging to the artists. Julian stood and listened. There was no sound of anyone in the room. Should he just take a

quick look round, and see if those lost papers were anywhere about?

Then he remembered the other four, waiting
patiently below in the cold. He had better go and tell
them what had happened. They could all come and
help in the search.

He stepped into the space behind the sliding back.
The sliding door slipped across again, and Julian was
left standing on the narrow ledge, with the old oak
door wide open to one side of him. He did not bother
to shut it. He felt about his feet, and found the iron
staples in the hole below him. Down he went, cling-
ing with his hands and feet, his torch in his teeth
again.

'Julian! What a time you've been! Quick, tell us all
about it!' cried George.

'It's most terribly thrilling,' said Julian. 'Absolutely
super! Where do you suppose all this leads to? Into the
cupboard at Kirrin Farmhouse – the one that's got a
false back!'

'Golly!' said Dick.

'I *say!*' said George.

'Did you go into the room?' cried Anne.

'I climbed as far as I could and came to a big oak
door,' said Julian. 'It has a handle this side, so I swung
it wide open. Then I saw another wooden door in front
of me – at least, I thought it was a door, I didn't know it
was just the false back of that cupboard. It was quite
easy to slide back and I stepped through, and found
myself among a whole lot of clothes hanging in the
cupboard! Then I hurried back to tell you.'

'Julian! We can hunt for those papers now,' said
George, eagerly. 'Was there anyone in the room?'

'I couldn't *hear* anyone,' said Julian. 'Now what I
propose is this – we'll all go up, and have a hunt round

those two rooms. The men have the room next to the cupboard one too.'

'Oh good!' said Dick, thrilled at the thought of such an adventure. 'Let's go now. You go first, Ju. Then Anne, then George and then me.'

'What about Tim?' asked George.

'He can't climb, silly,' said Julian. 'He's a simply marvellous dog, but he certainly can't climb, George. We'll have to leave him down here.'

'He won't like that,' said George.

'Well, we can't carry him up,' said Dick. 'You won't mind staying here for a bit, will you, Tim, old fellow?'

Tim wagged his tail. But, as he saw the four children mysteriously disappearing up the wall, he put his big tail down at once. What! Going without him? How could they?

He jumped up at the wall, and fell back. He jumped again and whined. George called down in a low voice.

'Be quiet, Tim dear! We shan't be long.'

Tim stopped whining. He lay down at the bottom of the wall, his ears well-cocked. This adventure was becoming more and more peculiar!

Soon the children were on the narrow ledge. The old oak door was still wide open. Julian shone his torch and the others saw the false back of the cupboard. Julian put his hands on it and it slid silently sideways. Then the torch shone on coats and dressing-gowns!

The children stood quite still, listening. There was no sound from the room. 'I'll open the cupboard door and peep into the room,' whispered Julian. 'Don't make a sound!'

The boy pushed between the clothes and felt for the outer cupboard door with his hand. He found it, and pushed it slightly. It opened a little and a shaft

of daylight came into the cupboard. He peeped
cautiously into the room.

There was no one there at all. That was good.
'Come on!' he whispered to the others. 'The room's
empty!'

One by one the children crept out of the clothes
cupboard and into the room. There was a big bed
there, a wash-stand, chest of drawers, small table and
two chairs. Nothing else. It would be easy to search
the whole room.

'Look, Julian, there's a door between the two
rooms,' said George, suddenly. 'Two of us can go and
hunt there and two here – and we can lock the doors
that lead on to the landing, so that no one can come in
and catch us!'

'Good idea!' said Julian, who was afraid that at any
moment someone might come in and catch them in
their search. 'Anne and I will go into the next room,
and you and Dick can search this one. Lock the door
that opens on to the landing, Dick, and I'll lock the one
in the other room. We'll leave the connecting-door
open, so that we can whisper to one another.'

Quietly the boy and girl slipped through the connecting-door into the second room, which was very
like the first. That was empty too. Julian went over to
the door that led to the landing, and turned the key in
the lock. He heard Dick doing the same to the door in
the other room. He heaved a big sigh. Now he felt
safe!

'Anne, turn up the rugs and see if any papers are
hidden there,' he said. 'Then look under the chair-
cushions and strip the bed to see if anything is hidden
under the mattress.'

Anne set to work, and Julian began to hunt too. He
started on the chest of drawers, which he thought

would be a very likely place to hide things in. The children's hands were shaking, as they felt here and there for the lost papers. It was so terribly exciting.

They wondered where the two men were. Down in the warm kitchen, perhaps. It was cold up here in the bedrooms, and they would not want to be away from the warmth. They could not go out because the snow was piled in great drifts round Kirrin Farmhouse!

Dick and George were searching hard in the other room. They looked in every drawer. They stripped the bed. They turned up rugs and carpet. They even put their hands up the big chimney-place!

'Julian? Have you found anything?' asked Dick in a low voice, appearing at the door between the two rooms.

'Not a thing,' said Julian, rather gloomily. 'They've hidden the papers well! I only hope they haven't got them on them – in their pockets, or something!'

Dick stared at him in dismay. He hadn't thought of that. 'That *would* be sickening!' he said.

'You go back and hunt *everywhere* – simply *everywhere!*' ordered Julian. 'Punch the pillows to see if they've stuck them under the pillow-case!'

Dick disappeared. Rather a lot of noise came from his room. It sounded as if he were doing a good deal of punching!

Anne and Julian went on hunting too. There was simply nowhere that they did not look. They even turned the pictures round to see if the papers had been stuck behind one of them. But there was nothing to be found. It was bitterly disappointing.

'We can't go without finding them,' said Julian, in desperation. 'It was such a bit of luck to get here like this, down the Secret Way – right into the bedrooms! We simply *must* find those papers!'

'I say,' said Dick, appearing again, 'I can hear voices! Listen!'

All four children listened. Yes – there were men's voices – just outside the bedroom doors!

16 The children are discovered

'What shall we do?' whispered George. They had all tiptoed to the first room, and were standing together, listening.

'We'd better go down the Secret Way again,' said Julian.

'Oh no, we . . .' began George, when she heard the handle of the door being turned. Whoever was trying to get in, could not open the door. There was an angry exclamation, and then the children heard Mr Wilton's voice. 'My door seems to have stuck. Do you mind If I come through your bedroom and see what's the matter with this handle?'

'Come right along!' came the voice of Mr Thomas. There was the sound of footsteps going to the outer door of the second room. Then there was the noise of a handle being turned and shaken.

'What's this!' said Mr Wilton, in exasperation. 'This won't open, either. Can the doors be locked?'

'It looks like it!' said Mr Thomas.

There was a pause. Then the children distinctly heard a few words uttered in a low voice. 'Are the papers safe? Is anyone after them?'

'They're in your room, aren't they?' said Mr Thomas. There was another pause. The children looked at one another. So the men *had* got the papers – and what was more, they *were* in the room! The very room the children stood in! They looked round it eagerly, racking their brains to think of some place they had not yet explored.

'Quick! Hunt round again while we've time,' whispered Julian. 'Don't make a noise.'

On tiptoe the children began a thorough hunt once more. How they searched! They even opened the pages of the books on the table, thinking that the papers might have been slipped in there. But they could find nothing.

'Hi, Mrs Sanders!' came Mr Wilton's voice. 'Have you by any chance locked these two doors? We can't get in!'

'Dear me!' said the voice of Mrs Sanders from the stairs. 'I'll come along and see. I certainly haven't locked any doors!'

Once again the handles were turned, but the doors would not open. The men began to get very impatient.

'Do you suppose anyone is in our rooms?' Mr Wilton asked Mrs Sanders.

She laughed.

'Well now, who would be in your rooms? There's only me and Mr Sanders in the house, and you know as well as I do that no one can come in from outside, for we're quite snowed up. I don't understand it – the locks of the doors must have slipped.'

Anne was lifting up the wash-stand jug to look underneath, at that moment. It was heavier than she thought, and she had to let it down again suddenly. It struck the marble wash-stand with a crash, and water slopped out all over the place!

Everyone outside the door heard the noise. Mr Wilton banged on the door and rattled the handle.

'Who's there? Let us in or you'll be sorry! What are you doing in there?'

'Idiot, Anne!' said Dick. 'Now they'll break the door down!'

That was exactly what the two men intended to do! Afraid that someone was mysteriously in their room, trying to find the stolen papers, they went quite mad, and began to put their shoulders to the door, and heave hard. The door shook and creaked.

'Now you be careful what you're doing!' cried the indignant voice of Mrs Sanders. The men took no notice. There came a crash as they both tried out their double strength on the door.

'Quick! We must go!' said Julian. 'We mustn't let the men know how we got here, or we shan't be able to come and hunt another time. Anne, George, Dick – get back to the cupboard quickly!'

The children raced for the clothes cupboard. 'I'il go first and help you down,' said Julian. He got out on to the narrow ledge and found the iron foot-holds with his feet. Down he went, torch held between his teeth as usual.

'Anne, come next,' he called. 'And Dick, you come third, and give a hand to Anne if she wants it. George is a good climber – she can easily get down herself.'

Anne was slow at climbing down. She was terribly excited, rather frightened, and so afraid of falling that she hardly dared to feel for each iron staple as she went down.

'Buck up, Anne!' whispered Dick, above her. 'The men have almost got the door down!'

There were tremendous sounds coming from the bedroom door. At any moment now it might break down, and the men would come racing in. Dick was thankful when he could begin to climb down the wall! Once they were all out, George could shut the big oak door, and they would be safe.

George was hidden among the clothes in the cupboard, waiting her turn to climb down. As she stood there, trying in vain to go over any likely hiding-place in her mind, her hands felt something rustly in the pocket of a coat she was standing against. It was a macintosh coat, with big pockets. The little girl's heart gave a leap.

Suppose the papers had been left in the pocket of the coat the man had on when he took them from Mr Roland? That was the only place the children had not searched – the pockets of the coats in the cupboard! With trembling fingers the girl felt in the pocket where the rustling was.

She drew out a sheaf of papers. It was dark in the cupboard, and she could not see if they were the ones she was hunting for, or not – but how she hoped they were! She stuffed them up the front of her jersey, for she had no big pocket, and whispered to Dick:

'Can I come now?'

CRASH! The door fell in with a terrific noise, and the two men leapt into the room. They looked round. It was empty! But there was the water spilt on the wash-stand and on the floor. Someone must be there somewhere!

'Look in the cupboard!' said Mr Thomas.

George crept out of the clothes cupboard and on to the narrow ledge, beyond the place where the false back of the cupboard used to be. It was still hidden sideways in the wall. The girl climbed down the hole a few steps and then shut the oak door which was now above her head. She had not enough strength to close it completely, but she hoped that now she was safe!

The men went to the cupboard and felt about in the clothes for anyone who might possibly be hiding there. Mr Wilton gave a loud cry.

'The papers are gone! They were in this pocket! There's not a sign of them. Quick, we must find the thief and get them back!'

The men did not notice that the cupboard seemed to go farther back than usual. They stepped away from it now that they were sure no one was there, and began to hunt round the room.

By now all the children except George were at the bottom of the hole, standing in the Secret Way, waiting impatiently for George to come down. Poor George was in such a hurry to get down that she caught her clothing on one of the staples, and had to stand in a very dangerous position trying to disentangle it.

'Come on, George, for goodness' sake!' said Julian.

Timothy jumped up at the wall. He could feel the fear and excitement of the waiting children, and it upset him. He wanted George. Why didn't she come? Why was she up that dark hole? Tim was unhappy about her.

He threw back his head and gave such a loud and mournful howl that all the children jumped violently.

'Shut up, Tim!' said Julian.

Tim howled again, and the weird sound echoed round and about in a strange manner. Anne was terrified, and she began to cry. Timothy howled again and again. Once he began to howl it was difficult to stop him.

The men in the bedroom above heard the extraordinary noise, and stopped in amazement.

'Whatever's that?' said one.

'Sounds like a dog howling in the depths of the earth,' said the other.

'Funny!' said Mr Wilton. 'It seems to be coming from the direction of that cupboard.'

He went over to it and opened the door. Tim chose that moment to give a specially mournful howl, and Mr Wilton jumped. He got into the cupboard and felt about at the back. The oak door there gave way beneath his hand, and he felt it open.

'There's something weird here,' called Mr Wilton. 'Bring my torch off the table.'

Tim howled again and the noise made Mr Wilton shiver! Tim had a peculiarly horrible howl. It came echoing up the hole, and burst out into the cupboard.

Mr Thomas got the torch. The men shone it at the back of the cupboard, and gave an exclamation.

'Look at that! There's a door here! Where does it lead to?'

Mrs Sanders, who had been watching everything in surprise and indignation, angry that her door should have been broken down, came up to the cupboard.

'My!' she said. 'I knew there was a false back to that cupboard – but I didn't know there was another door behind it too! That must be the entrance to the Secret Way that people used in the old days.'

'Where does it lead to?' rapped out Mr Wilton.

'Goodness knows!' said Mrs Sanders. 'I never took much interest in such things.'

'Come on, we must go down,' said Mr Wilton, shining his torch into the square black hole, and seeing the iron foot-holds set in the stone. 'This is where the thief went. He can't have got far. We'll go after him. We've got to get those papers back!'

It was not long before the two men had swung themselves over the narrow ledge and down into the hole, feeling with their feet for the iron staples. Down they went and down, wondering where they were coming to. There was no sound below them. Clearly the thief had got away!

George had got down at last. Tim almost knocked her over in his joy. She put her hand on his head. 'You old silly!' she said. 'I believe you've given our secret away! Quick, Ju – we must go, because those men will be after us in a minute. They could easily hear Tim's howling!'

Julian took Anne's hand. 'Come along, Anne,' he said. 'You must run as fast as you can. Hurry now! Dick, keep with George.'

The four of them hurried down the dark, narrow passage. What a long way they had to go home! If only the passage wasn't such a long one! The children's hearts were beating painfully as they made haste, stumbling as they went.

Julian shone his light steadily in front of him, and Dick shone his at the back. Half-leading, half-dragging Anne, Julian hurried along. Behind them they heard a shout.

'Look! There's a light ahead! That's the thief! Come on, we'll soon get him!'

17 Good old Tim!

'Hurry, Anne. Do hurry!' shouted Dick, who was just behind.

Poor Anne was finding it very difficult to get along quickly. Pulled by Julian and pushed by Dick, she almost fell two or three times. Her breath came in loud pants, and she felt as if she would burst.

'Let me have a rest!' she panted. But there was no time for that, with the two men hurrying after them! They came to the piece that was widened out, where the rocky bench was, and Anne looked longingly at it. But the boys hurried her on.

Suddenly the little girl caught her foot on a stone and fell heavily, almost dragging Julian down with her. She tried to get up, and began to cry.

'I've hurt my foot! I've twisted it! Oh, Julian, it hurts me to walk.'

'Well, you've just *got* to come along, darling,' said Julian, sorry for his little sister, but knowing that they would all be caught if he was not firm. 'Hurry as much as you can.'

But now it was impossible for Anne to go fast. She cried with pain as her foot hurt her, and hobbled along so slowly that Dick almost fell over her. Dick cast a look behind him and saw the light of the men's torches coming nearer and nearer. Whatever were they to do?

'I'll stay here with Tim and keep them off,' said George, suddenly. 'Here, take these papers, Dick! I believe they're the ones we want, but I'm not sure till we get a good light to see them. I found them in a pocket of one of the coats in the cupboard.'

'Golly!' said Dick, surprised. He took the sheaf of papers and stuffed them up his jersey, just as George had stuffed them up hers. They were too big to go into his trouser pockets. 'I'll stay with you, George, and let the other two go on ahead.'

'No. I want the papers taken to safety, in case they are my father's,' said George. 'Go on, Dick! I'll be all right here with Tim. I shall stay here just where the passage curves round this rocky bit. I'll make Tim bark like mad.'

'Suppose the men have got revolvers?' said Dick, doubtfully. 'They might shoot him.'

'I bet they haven't,' said George. '*Do* go, Dick! The men are almost here. There's the light of their torch.'

Dick sped after the stumbling Anne. He told Julian what George had suggested. 'Good for George!' said Julian. 'She really is marvellous – not afraid of anything! She will keep the men off till I get poor old Anne back.'

George was crouching behind the rocky bit, her hand on Tim's collar, waiting. 'Now, Tim!' she whispered. 'Bark your loudest. Now!'

Timothy had been growling up till now, but at George's command he opened his big mouth and barked. How he barked! He had a simply enormous voice, and the barks went echoing all down the dark and narrow passage. The hurrying men, who were near the rocky piece of the passage, stopped.

'If you come round this bend, I'll set my dog on you!' cried George.

'It's a child shouting,' said one man to another. 'Only a child! Come on!'

Timothy barked again, and pulled at his collar. He was longing to get at the men. The light of their torch shone round the bend. George let Tim go, and the big dog sprang joyfully round the curve to meet his enemies.

They suddenly saw him by the light of their torch, and he was a very terrifying sight! To begin with, he was a big dog, and now that he was angry all the hairs on the back of his neck had risen up, making him look even more enormous. His teeth were bared and glinted in the torch-light.

The men did not like the look of him at all. 'If you move one step nearer I'll tell my dog to fly at you!' shouted George. 'Wait, Tim, wait! Stand there till I give the word.'

The dog stood in the light of the torch, growling deeply. He looked an extremely fierce animal. The men looked at him doubtfully. One man took a step forward and George heard him. At once she shouted to Tim.

'Go for him, Tim, go for him!'

Tim leapt at the man's throat. He took him completely by surprise and the man fell to the ground with a thud, trying to beat off the dog. The other man helped.

'Call off your dog or we'll hurt him!' cried the second man.

'It's much more likely he'll hurt *you*!' said George, coming out from behind the rock and enjoying the fun. 'Tim, come off.'

Tim came away from the man he was worrying, looking up at his mistress as if to say, 'I was having *such* a good time! Why did you spoil it?'

'Who are you?' said the man on the ground.

'I'm not answering any of your questions,' said

George. 'Go back to Kirrin Farmhouse, that's my advice to you. If you dare to come along this passage I'll set my dog on to you again – and next time he'll do more damage.'

The men turned and went back the way they had come. They neither of them wanted to face Tim again. George waited until she could no longer see the light of their torch, then she bent down and patted Timothy.

'Brave, good dog!' she said. 'I love you, darling Tim, and you don't know how proud I am of you! Come along – we'll hurry after the others now. I expect those two men will explore this passage some time tonight, and won't they get a shock when they find out where it leads to, and see who is waiting for them!'

George hurried along the rest of the long passage, with Tim running beside her. She had Dick's torch, and it did not take her long to catch the others up. She panted out to them what had happened, and even poor Anne chuckled in delight when she heard how Tim had flung Mr Wilton to the ground.

'Here we are,' said Julian, as the passage came to a stop below the hole in the study floor. 'Hallo – what's this?'

A bright light was shining down the hole, and the rug and carpet, so carefully pulled over the hole by Julian, were now pulled back again. The children gazed up in surprise.

Uncle Quentin was there, and Aunt Fanny, and when they saw the children's faces looking up at them from the hole, they were so astonished that they very nearly fell down the hole too!

'Julian! Anne! What in the wide world are you doing down there?' cried Uncle Quentin. He gave them each a hand up, and the four children and Timothy were at last safe in the warm study. How good it was to feel warm again! They got as near the fire as they could.

'Children – what *is* the meaning of this?' asked Aunt Fanny. She looked white and worried. 'I came into the study to do some dusting, and when I stood on that bit of the rug, it seemed to give way beneath me. When I pulled it up and turned back the carpet, I saw that hole – and the hole in the panelling too! And then I found that all of you had disappeared, and went to fetch your uncle. What *has* been happening – and where does that hole lead to?'

Dick took the sheaf of papers from under his jersey and gave them to George. She took them and handed them to her father. 'Are these the missing pages?' she asked.

Her father fell on them as if they had been worth more than a hundred times their weight in gold. 'Yes! Yes! They're the pages – all three of them! Thank goodness they're back. They took me three years to bring to perfection, and contained the heart of my secret formula. George, where did you get them?'

'It's a very long story,' said George. 'You tell it all, Julian, I feel tired.'

Julian began to tell the tale. He left out nothing. He told how George had found Mr Roland snooping about the study – how she had felt sure that the tutor had not wanted Timmy in the house because the dog gave warning of his movements at night – how George had seen him talking to the two artists, although he had said he did not know them. As the tale went on, Uncle Quentin and Aunt Fanny looked more and more amazed. They simply could not believe it all.

But after all, there were the missing papers, safely back. That was marvellous. Uncle Quentin hugged the papers as if they were a precious baby. He would not put them down for a moment.

George told the bit about Timmy keeping the men off the escaping children. 'So you see, although you made poor Tim live out in the cold, away from me, he really saved us all, and your papers too,' she said to her father, fixing her brilliant blue eyes on him.

Her father looked most uncomfortable. He felt very guilty for having punished George and Timothy. They had been right about Mr Roland and he had been wrong.

'Poor George,' he said, 'and poor Timmy. I'm sorry about all that.'

George did not bear malice once anyone had owned themselves to be in the wrong. She smiled at her father.

'It's all right,' she said. 'But don't you think that as I was punished unfairly, Mr Roland might be punished well and truly? He deserves it!'

'Oh, he shall be, certainly he shall be,' promised her father. 'He's up in bed with a cold, as you know. I hope he doesn't hear any of this, or he may try to escape.'

'He can't,' said George. 'We're snowed up. You could ring up the police, and arrange for them to come here as soon as ever they can manage it, when the snow has cleared. And I rather think those other two men will try to explore the Secret Way as soon as possible, to get the papers back. Could we catch them when they arrive, do you think?'

'Rather!' said Uncle Quentin, though Aunt Fanny looked as if she didn't want any more exciting things to happen! 'Now look here, you seem really frozen all of you, and you must be hungry too, because it's almost lunch-time. Go into the dining-room and sit by the fire, and Joanna shall bring us all a hot lunch. Then we'll talk about what to do.'

Nobody said a word to Mr Roland, of course. He lay in bed, coughing now and then. George had slipped up and locked his door. She wasn't going to have him wandering out and overhearing anything!

They all enjoyed their hot lunch, and became warm and cosy. It was nice to sit there together, talking over their adventure, and planning what to do.

'I will telephone to the police, of course,' said Uncle Quentin. 'And tonight we will put Timmy into the study to give the two artists a good welcome if they arrive!'

Mr Roland was most annoyed to find his door locked that afternoon when he took it into his head to dress and go downstairs. He banged on it indignantly. George grinned and went upstairs. She had told the other children how she had locked the door.

'What's the matter, Mr Roland?' she asked, in a polite voice.

'Oh, it's you, George, is it?' said the tutor. 'See what's the matter with my door, will you? I can't open it.'

George had pocketed the key when she had locked the door. She answered Mr Roland in a cheerful voice.

'Oh Mr Roland, there's no key in your door, so I can't unlock it. I'll see if I can find it!'

Mr Roland was angry and puzzled. He couldn't understand why his door was locked and the key gone. He did not guess that everyone knew about him now. Uncle Quentin laughed when George went down and told him about the locked door.

'He may as well be kept a prisoner,' he said. 'He can't escape now.'

That night, everyone went to bed early, and Timmy

was left in the study, guarding the hole. Mr Roland had become more and more angry and puzzled when his door was not unlocked. He had shouted for Uncle Quentin, but only George had come. He could not understand it. George, of course, was enjoying herself. She made Timothy bark outside Mr Roland's door, and this puzzled him too, for he knew that George was not supposed to see Timmy for three days. Wild thoughts raced through his head. Had that fierce, impossible child locked up her father and mother and Joanna, as well as himself? He could not imagine what had happened.

In the middle of the night Timmy awoke everyone by barking madly. Uncle Quentin and the children hurried downstairs, followed by Aunt Fanny, and the amazed Joanna. A fine sight met their eyes!

Mr Wilton and Mr Thomas were in the study crouching behind the sofa, terrified of Timothy, who was barking for all he was worth! Timmy was standing by the hole in the stone floor, so that the two men could not escape down there. Artful Timmy! He had waited in silence until the men had crept up the hole into the study, and were exploring it, wondering where they were – and then the dog had leapt to the hole to guard it, preventing the men from escaping.

'Good evening, Mr Wilton, good evening, Mr Thomas,' said George, in a polite voice. 'Have you come to see our tutor Mr Roland?'

'So this is where he lives!' said Mr Wilton. 'Was it you in the passage today?'

'Yes – and my cousins,' said George. 'Have you come to look for the papers you stole from my father?'

The two men were silent. They knew they were caught. Mr Wilton spoke after a moment.

'Where's Mr Roland?'

'Shall we take these men to Mr Roland, Uncle?' asked Julian, winking at George. 'Although it's in the middle of the night I'm sure he would love to see them.'

'Yes,' said his uncle, jumping at once to what the boy meant to do. 'Take them up. Timmy, you go too.'

The men followed Julian upstairs, Timmy close at their heels. George followed too, grinning. She handed Julian the key. He unlocked the door and the men went in, just as Julian switched on the light. Mr Roland was wide awake and gave an exclamation of complete amazement when he saw his friends.

Before they had time to say a word Julian locked the door again and threw the key to George.

'A nice little bag of prisoners,' he said. 'We will leave old Tim outside the door to guard them. It's impossible to get out of that window, and anyway, we're snowed up if they could escape that way.'

Everyone went to bed again, but the children found it difficult to sleep after such an exciting time. Anne and George whispered together and so did Julian and Dick. There was such a lot to talk about.

Next day there was a surprise for everyone. The police did arrive after all! The snow did not stop them, for somewhere or other they had got skis and had come skimming along valiantly to see the prisoners! It was a great excitement for everyone.

'We won't take the men away, sir, till the snow has gone,' said the Inspector. 'We'll just put the handcuffs on them, so that they don't try any funny tricks. You keep the door locked too, and that dog outside. They'll be safe there for a day or two. We've taken them enough food till we come back again. If they go a bit short, it will serve them right!'

The snow melted two days later, and the police

took away Mr Roland and the others. The children watched.

'No more lessons *these* hols!' said Anne gleefully.

'No more shutting Timothy out of the house,' said George.

'You were right and we were wrong, George,' said Julian. 'You were fierce, weren't you?—but it's a jolly good thing you were!'

'She *is* fierce, isn't she?' said Dick, giving the girl a sudden hug. 'But I rather like her when she's fierce, don't you, Julian? Oh George, we do have marvellous adventures with you! I wonder if we'll have any more?'

They will—there isn't a doubt of that!

The Enid Blyton Newsletter

Would you like to receive the Enid Blyton Newsletter? It has lots of news about Enid Blyton books, videos, plays, etc. There are also puzzles and a page for your letters. It is published three times a year and is free for children who live in the United Kingdom and Ireland.

If you would like to receive it for a year, please write to: The Enid Blyton Newsletter, PO Box 357, London WC2E 9HQ, sending your name and address. (UK and Ireland only)

A complete list of the FAMOUS FIVE
ADVENTURES *by Enid Blyton*

1 FIVE ON A TREASURE ISLAND
2 FIVE GO ADVENTURING AGAIN
3 FIVE RUN AWAY TOGETHER
4 FIVE GO TO SMUGGLER'S TOP
5 FIVE GO OFF IN A CARAVAN
6 FIVE ON KIRRIN ISLAND AGAIN
7 FIVE GO OFF TO CAMP
8 FIVE GET INTO TROUBLE
9 FIVE FALL INTO ADVENTURE
10 FIVE ON A HIKE TOGETHER
11 FIVE HAVE A WONDERFUL TIME
12 FIVE GO DOWN TO THE SEA
13 FIVE GO TO MYSTERY MOOR
14 FIVE HAVE PLENTY OF FUN
15 FIVE ON A SECRET TRAIL
16 FIVE GO TO BILLYCOCK HILL
17 FIVE GET INTO A FIX
18 FIVE ON FINNISTON FARM
19 FIVE GO TO DEMON'S ROCKS
20 FIVE HAVE A MYSTERY TO SOLVE
21 FIVE ARE TOGETHER AGAIN

A complete list of the SECRET SEVEN
ADVENTURES *by Enid Blyton*

Have you played any of these exciting
Hodder Children's Books Adventure Game books?

FAMOUS FIVE ADVENTURE GAMES:
THE WRECKERS' TOWER GAME
THE HAUNTED RAILWAY GAME
THE WHISPERING ISLAND GAME
THE SINISTER LAKE GAME
THE WAILING LIGHTHOUSE GAME
THE SECRET AIRFIELD GAME
THE SHUDDERING MOUNTAIN GAME
THE MISSING SCIENTIST GAME

ASTERIX ADVENTURE GAMES:
ASTERIX TO THE RESCUE
OPERATION BRITAIN

THE PETER PAN ADVENTURE GAME:
PETER'S REVENGE

BIGGLES ADVENTURE GAMES:
THE SECRET NIGHT FLYER GAME
THE HIDDEN BLUEPRINTS GAME

THE FOOTBALL ADVENTURE GAME:
TACTICS!

GHOST ADVENTURE GAMES:
GHOSTLY TOWERS
GHOST TRAIN